Jubilee King

Jubilee King

stories

JESSE SHEPARD

BLOOMSBURY

For Maura

My thanks to Amy, Melissa, and Colin for their
hard work, my mother O-Lan, my father Sam, and
Scarlett and John for their encouragement.

Published by Bloomsbury, New York and London
Distributed to the trade by Holtzbrinck Publishers

Library of Congress Cataloging-in-Publication Data has been
applied for.

ISBN: 1-58234-340-3

First U.S. Edition 2003

10 9 8 7 6 5 4 3 2 1

Typeset by Palimpsest Book Production Limited,
Polmont, Stirlingshire, Scotland
Printed in the United States of America
by R.R. Donnelly & Sons, Crawfordsville

Contents

First Day She'd Never See

Everything hinges on selling the Plymouth. I've got to get rid of this Valiant. I've had a few people come over and look at the For Sale sign I made with cardboard and a permanent marker. They cup their hands and look in at the interior. When they see I'm living in the backseat, they get spooked. I roll down the window, and they take steps backward. It might be my beard, I don't know. I say, "You interested?" I soften my voice and smile, but they walk away and chuckle to their girlfriends. The girlfriends are usually the ones interested in the car, they think it's funky or cute. I hear them talking when they walk back to their Nissans or to the new coffee shop next to Life Foods here in the Vintner's Plaza parking lot.

I used to park on Limber Street under an acacia tree. Everyone avoided the tree – yellow pods dropped and powdered their pristine paint jobs, so the spot was always open. The droppings gave me good cover. I was safe in there. The mustard-colored silt caked all the windows and blended with the butter-yellow paint of the Plymouth. It could have been any abandoned car. But then reverse went out, and parallel parking became impossible. I'm not going to push the thing around, so I had to move out here to the Vintner's Plaza parking lot where I can always be nosed out.

I don't see a big problem not going backward as long as I plan ahead. Gas stations can be tricky, or if I was in the city, parking would be a bitch, but out here in the valley I don't really miss it. As long as I remember I can *only* go forward, I can do away with the luxury of reverse. It's a selling point, really, a car that will only go forward. No one seems to see it that way, but I'm only asking $500 for the thing.

The Vintner's Plaza parking lot is big enough to hide a fleet of ships – planter-box islands, sod medians, benches, fountains. Whoever designed this lot had a big American idea of adventure in parking. They didn't think the shops would be alluring enough, maybe, and had to create a mad landscaped labyrinth of parking areas to keep the consumers entertained.

The pine-tree grove on the south side with its tan bark and little hilly pathways seems especially attractive to the Jeeps and Explorers, a pseudorustic escape from the multilevel parking structure downtown. Hondas, Volkswagens, and convertible coupes lean toward the tropical palm-tree islands on the north end. The Lincolns, Buicks, and Cadillacs don't seem to mind the central wide-open parking – those people just want to get in, shop, and get out. But the BMWs, Lexuses, Jaguars – they're all shining by the fountain in front of the new coffee shop, shining like they just had their teeth done.

The new coffee shop is one of those chain cafés that tries to outdo their competition with ridiculous variations on the word *Java*. This one's called ¡Mo'Java!, with an inverted exclamation mark and gaudy multicolored lettering. Things here are a lot different than the Salvation Army rehab outside town; I checked in there when I first moved up from San Rafael a year ago.

The facility was a winery-resort–type hotel in the seventies, but it had transformed into a burned-out haven for users by the time I got there – paint over the wallpaper, gray indoor/outdoor carpet on the wood floors. It's strange how people go out of their way to make a nice place bleak; none of us had a chance of seeing our lives any better. They gave us projects, though, the social workers; they made us work. We moved junked lawn mowers and vacuum cleaners, fire-hazard appliances, and countless boxes of clothes and bric-a-brac that all smelled like it had been through a bayou flood. The smell was always the same no matter where in the county it had come from or how much cologne or perfume or fabric softener or syrup or

God knows what suburban odor of kids and puke and
cigarettes had lived on the stuff – it all mixed together in
the same germ-infested stink of a rank garage sale. I couldn't
get away from the smell – it saturated everything for the
month I was there.

There didn't seem much sense in moving all the donated
stuff from the trucks it came in on to the work yard, to the
storage sites, to the sale yard, then back to the trucks that
then took it all to the dump. Some of the crap managed to
sell to the strange dirty regulars that made shrieking family
excursions out of shopping the sale yard. I'd see the same
families digging through the nasty boxes of shit, handing a
broken Nerf gun to their grubby toddlers to shut them up or
trying to start a chain saw that'd been in a creek for a month.
They never bought much, those people, but they always
came back like they might find a real treasure, something
we'd overlooked. The work kept us busy anyway – better
busy than idle when every minute is a long day. But now
I'm on my own, straight, just me and the Plymouth and the
Vintner's Plaza lot.

More people in white shorts today – I've counted twenty
already and it's only noon. No potential buyers yet, though –
nobody that would even notice my Plymouth. These are the
same types of people that were at the golf course, Sonoma
County elite in white shorts.

I filled the range-ball machine at the Sweetcreek Golf
Course for a while after rehab. I didn't go out in the tractor

and actually retrieve the balls – you have to work your way up to that. Hipolito was the guy who drove the retriever, the "Lab," I called it, like a Labrador retriever. Hipolito didn't get the pun.

Spring weekends were the worst at the range. Everybody came out with the good weather, and the balls would be flying like hail out there. I'd be dumping buckets of balls into the machine, and Hipolito would be picking them up. I'd see him hauling ass across the driving range, balls dinging off the cage. He never flinched when the balls hit the Lab. He'd come in with a load, then go back out. I'd hustle to keep the machine full, wondering why the course couldn't afford more balls so we didn't have to work so hard. It was a primitive system. Then the machine would jam up – always when we were busy – and we'd have a line of these Sonoma County people waiting in their goofy golf outfits complaining. That pissed Hipolito off, and he'd yell at me as if I'd made the machine jam. He'd say, "God fuckit, Saymone!" That's how he pronounced my name: *Saymone*. He couldn't wrap his accent around "Simon." He cursed the same way, always a little off like "God fuckit" or "Hell shit." I laughed the first few times I heard him curse in English, but that just made him rattle off some long Spanish language that I'm sure he had right.

I was fired after they discovered I was living in their parking lot, my "home on the *range*," I called it. Hipolito didn't get that either. They found out I was living in my car around the same time the range-ball machine came up short on cash. They put it on me, not the piece-of-shit machine or Hipolito. I'm sure Hipolito lightened the till, but I didn't hold a grudge.

Sweetcreek people don't have much tolerance for anybody who isn't an architect or a vintner or some Silicon Valley high roller. People here need the cheap Mexican labor, but they treat immigrants like shit. They find some place in their heart for a stray dog that's pulled free of its tree, but a "destitute Caucasian transient" (like they called me in the *Sweetcreek Tribune*) just doesn't have a place. The incident of the range-ball machine made the *Tribune,* if that's any indication of the lives these people have.

There's a sucker's hole in the storm front today that's bringing all these idiots out in their shorts, typical California visitors that haven't been through a spring here. They figure the rain's a fluke in their idea of the "wine country," and now they'll be stuck in the wrong apparel twenty miles from their bed-and-breakfasts. Like the guy I see now across the parking lot, his legs sticking out like summer sausages. He's with his daughter in front of the coffee shop sucking on lattes or something. The daughter looks all right, forced to make the trip with Pops. She's at that prime "just got my license" age and can spot a For Sale sign on a windshield a hundred yards away.

Yeah, you like the car, don't you, you little peach? You

think it's funky. You want to be the type of girl who drives a '69 Valiant. You could pack all your tight-assed girlfriends in here, couldn't you? Just have a rebellious little sorority adventure . . .

That's right, babe, convince Daddy you need to look at the Valiant. It's a safe car, a practical car.

You've got him lifting his sunglasses and looking. That's the way, use your charm.

Daddy's walking over! The guy's got to be 250, a hobbled, running walk like he's being tugged by his gut. Purple ACL scars stretch over his knees like night crawlers. He must've been a fullback thirty years ago, one of those "quick for a big man" types. Too bad about the knees.

"You sellin' this?" he asks me, exhaling nastily through his nose.

"Yes, sir. I'm Simon."

"Simon, Terrence. What is it, a Dart?" He doesn't offer a shake and keeps moving. Eye contact ain't his bag.

"Valiant," I tell him.

He paddles around the side, running his hand over the quarter panel.

The daughter waits at the coffee shop, watching us.

"How many miles?" Terrence asks, his questions ending in an upward tone swing each time.

"Hard to say," I tell him.

I open the hood for him, and he leans his Grecian Formula head in, like he can solve all my problems, like he invented the slant-six motor. His breathing is louder under the hood.

"You think it's going to clear up?" he asks me, stroking the long valve cover like a dachshund.

"What?"

"The weather . . ." he says, making a quick irritated hand movement, like he's got a bug at his ear. "You think it'll clear up?"

"It'll be clear up to our ass in a few minutes," I tell him. He chuckles, like I might be dangerous.

He takes the air cleaner off and fiddles with the carburetor.

"Is it in your name?" he asks me, interested.

"Yeah, it's in my name."

He pulls out the dipstick and smells the end of it. The oil puts a spot on his nose, and he swipes it off with another quick hand move.

"What's the history?" he asks, putting the dipstick back in.

"I've had it three years," I tell him.

The truth is more fucked than fiction when it comes down to it. Denice made me realize that. I see her hair when I think of her now. Three years. I see her hair, not her teeth or her tits or her scary pale eyes. I don't see the whole time we had in San Rafael, unless I let her hair take me there, and I have to stop thinking and distract myself with something like buttoning my coat against this weather that's coming in.

I used to call her a troll doll. She didn't like it the first time I called her that – too close to home, some home she had before I knew her, but when things were good she called herself a troll doll, like that was the only secret we had.

The description was right. Blond cords burst from her head in a dense bush of chaos – you wouldn't think her neck could support it. Her hair might've reached her ass if it were straight, but the kinky life in it kept it all aloft and her little body poked out underneath like a dandelion stem. There were lengthy washing and drying procedures, daylong events that coincided with her not going outside our apartment. I'd just pound the pavement for a while or go to a matinée on those days. They were always gloomy days, blustery she called them, days like today that forced their unmade-up mind on the county – sunny and raining, rainbows. Those days kept her bound to our one-room apartment.

"I can't go out in this!" Denice would say, pointing at the weather out our third-floor window. She'd look out at the wet fir trees beyond the street below, she'd look out at the mixed-up clouds above the hills, the drops of water on the windows, and then back at me.

"Why don't you get us some coffees and a *Times*," she'd say.

Her hair was her biggest asset and her biggest complaint. I'd watch her bind it back with industrial rubber bands, but it still made a run at the world. She wouldn't cut it. If she'd cut it, she would have had to find some other thing to be a burden.

I gave her an umbrella for Valentine's Day, a red one. She hated it.

"What's the real reason you don't go outside?" I asked her.

"Fuck off, Simon," she said.

I felt I was doing the right thing giving her the umbrella. Hats didn't come close to covering her head. I thought an umbrella would be a solution, but she saw it as an insult. I bought her a plane ticket to visit her mother in L.A. – she thought I was trying to get rid of her. I bought her a subscription to *Fitness* magazine, since she always peeked at it in the supermarket. She thought it implied she was out of shape.

"Is it my ass?" she said.

"Is what?" I said.

"You think I've got a fat ass?"

"I love your ass."

"Why did you get the subscription?"

"I thought you wanted it," I said.

"Bullshit!"

"Come on, Denice. This is ridiculous."

"What's ridiculous – that I don't bow down like some little bitch? Is that what's ridiculous, Simon?"

"It's turning into more than it should," I said.

"What should it be?"

"What?"

"What *should* this be, Simon?"

"It should be nothing! Simple. Nothing!"

"You want nothing, you've got it. You've got fucking nothing!"

I'd walk uptown to the Paper Ace for a cocktail. I'd walk through the wet sidewalk like my feet were on fire, breaking an aggravated sweat by the time I got to the bar.

"Can I look in the trunk?" Terrence asks me, walking to the back of the car.

"Sure," I tell him. "Your daughter interested in the car?"

"Well, yeah, she needs a car . . . depends what's wrong with it."

"Reverse won't engage." I tell him like it's not a big thing.

"Huh. Is that right?"

I can feel the deal slipping.

"It might be linkage, some adjustment," I say, feeling it may be the turning point.

My other girlfriends hadn't been as close up as Denice. That's how I think of her, close up, like she was in my clothes, like she had her hand in my crotch and my heart in her teeth. We made up. We made up with liquor and mad fucking against the bathroom door or in the closet, with all her pointed heels poking into us. We'd be sore and hungover and relieved for a day or two, sometimes a week. We'd walk through town holding hands like civilized lovers, talking in the plaza about some movie we'd seen or laughing at people that tripped on the high curbs. We wore sunglasses, and people admired us. We struck envy in our single friends. Then we'd slip.

We were into speed and booze. We'd huff lines of amphetamine and drive to the Paper Ace at night. We'd be shaking by the time we parked under the sycamore tree a block away. We'd abandon the closed-up space of the Plymouth and hike like escaped convicts toward the warm lights of the bar. We'd run across the inter-section, finding an excuse in the oncoming traffic to run to the bar. Our gums ached. We'd be giddy discussing the drinks we'd order, nearing the red swinging door that always glowed like an escape hatch from the stag-nance of San Rafael. We knew the bartenders. "Shit, it's a *Harold* night," we'd say, or "Hey, *Sonny's* working." We kept the barkeep guessing at our cocktails so they'd never serve us a usual. But they all knew us. Everyone knew us.

"No reverse, huh?" Terrence says, stepping back from the Valiant and standing still for the first time.

"It just won't engage, I don't know why," I tell him, hoping ignorance might be a positive thing. I know the transmission needs a rebuild, but that would cost more than the car's worth.

Terrence ponders the problem, not wanting to give up on it entirely.

"The car runs great otherwise." I tell him, "The electrical is A-one." It sounds fishy once I say it.

"A-one . . . Yeah, I don't know. It might be more than I want to get into."

"I can understand that, Terrence." Better to let him convince himself, maybe. The Plymouth has got him hooked in some way, though – the motor, he loves the motor.

"That slant-six is bulletproof," I tell him. "They pulled 'em off the line 'cause they lasted so long," I say, hoping for another chance.

"I know the motor, that ain't the problem. That motor will be ticking when we're *both* gone. But if the tranny's bad . . ."

He cocks his head and swipes at his ear again, a habit that now makes me wonder about its origin.

Denice got cold on the pool table. Her eyes turned hard, and she'd demand quiet without saying anything. Pale stress lines creased high on her cheeks when she lined up a shot. Her forehead would pinch in ridges, and she'd look old for a moment before making impact with the cue ball. If the shot went the way she meant, a white smile cut through her jungle hair. If she missed, the creases stayed under her eyes, and she'd quietly step away from the table.

Pool was our getaway car. We found something that turned us on to each other in the game – posture, determination, competitiveness. We never played each other. That turned bad. We'd watch each other play, and it was fantastic, fantastic in the way that screwing in front of a mirror was fantastic. We'd take more speed in the rest room and order more drinks. I'd grab her and hang on, hang on to her thick hair. Her eyes would drift, and I'd feel her be with me, a privilege in her closeness that made the envy of all the bar losers palpable. We'd play pool until closing, then try to make it home without crashing or fucking in the car.

Our daytime life lacked all that fantasy. Whatever pent-up passion we had came out stupidly brutal. We had to make it through the day to get to the Paper Ace.

"Will you take four hundred for it?" Terrence asks me from the driver's seat. He looks strangely delicate below me in my own car, like a ten-year-old boy with a slow metabolism.

"I'm really hoping for five," I tell him, seeing which way he'll go with it.

He looks over the dash, gripping the skinny steering wheel. He turns it back and forth.

"Maybe your daughter should drive it?" I suggest.

"Yeah," he says, relieved he doesn't have to get defensive about the price, maybe. He climbs out and does a slight variation of his hand flick toward his daughter. She picks up on the subtle motion at the coffee shop and starts walking over.

"You can always find parts for this car," I say.

"Yeah, yeah."

My sales pitch has dead-ended. He needs the daughter's convincing.

Denice wouldn't let me drive. "You're higher than the moon," she said. She was higher than the clouds, but that was better than the moon, I guess. Pre–full moon made us question mortality. We both reacted the same way to its brightness – we had to show respect in a certain madness of speed and drink.

She drove with all the cockiness of a woman being hit on by strange men. She drove with the recklessness of not being understood. Unabashed, accelerating in the side streets, being the car that blasts by on a quiet night, the car you hear from your bed that flies toward a turn on your street and locks up with badly balanced American steel and skinny tires to drift through and accelerate again.

"I'm jumping if you don't slow the fuck down!"

I said that. I yelled at her curly head, victim in my own Plymouth. I yelled my threat of self-sacrifice, but she just found octane in my helplessness.

That's how I saw her, laughing, rolling, hidden by her hair, driving.

Flinging my door out against the wind didn't slow her. Feeling my body make the dive didn't change her speed. I remember the sober coiled-up moment of hurtling into the street, the moment that curled me line-drive out of the Valiant, flying in a ball along the concrete: She'll know me now, she'll know me as a real man?

My doubt phrased it as a question on impact. The words came into my teeth with the concussion, spitting out with the strange mushroomy taste of collision. All I saw were the strip taillights of the Plymouth and her bloom of hair flashing in silhouette through the back window as the passenger door swung.

Denice never let off the gas. She drove on through the sycamore trees that lined the street, and vanished with just the sound of the exhaust fading.

I walked home, bruised, my knees on fire. I shuffled hard in the quiet of the bedtime houses that hid in the trees. I smoked a broken cigarette. I climbed the steep stairs to our apartment and screamed at the door. I kicked at the wood. I searched for keys that were inside already. She didn't let me in. I collapsed at our door and slept. Even in the erratic popping of my heart against my chest, I slept.

The daughter slips into the driver's seat without a care of the mechanics. She's starstruck by the Valiant.

"No reverse, hon," Terrence warns her.

"How funny," she says, climbing into the backseat. She

stretches her smooth legs out and crosses her arms under her breasts like she's on a dick-tease date.

"What's her name?" she asks me, shrugging her shoulders coltishly.

"What?"

"A car like this has to have a name," she says, climbing out.

"Uh, Denice," I tell her. "Her name's Denice."

"Denice," she says, shutting the heavy door. "I love it! I love it, Dad."

The first day Denice would never see came dark and hard – a day that took its coat off and spread out nude to rain on the world. A day she'd never go out in.

She was pregnant, he told me – the man who tested her blood. First trimester, he said, suspicion and sympathy in his professional voice.

I watched them emerge from the base of our staircase. I watched from the street, March rain hitting me in the back. The sheet didn't cover all of her hair.

Rain came on. I wanted to get the umbrella, the red umbrella. I had thoughts of sprinting up the staircase and searching the strange corners of our apartment, as if that duty might be the right thing to do, as if I would possibly be part of the right thing to do. But I only watched.

They loaded her onto the rain-cleaned ambulance. It didn't bother with its lights – there was no urgency any more. The medics loaded her in a slow-motion drill, as if prolonging the event showed more heart.

She'd been dead all night, while I slept outside the door. Her heart had failed. Her young heart failed her when it should have been charging at the world with the same tenacity as her hair, the crazy spring of life still in it when they drove away.

Terrence gives in to five hundred cash for the Valiant. I write up a bill of sale, the final deal strangely deflating. I count his ATM money – more than I've had in hand for years. The daughter runs a celebration lap around the car, squealing. She ends up at her dad and hugs him.

I unload my things. The blacktop starts to darken wet with the drizzle.

"You'll take care of her now?" I say to the girl, and she stares at me stunned, like the car is already hers, like she's owned it all along.

"Remember, you can only go forward," I tell her, stuffing my clothes into a jacket and tying the sleeves around them in a square knot. I swing the bundle over my shoulder and walk toward the eaves of Vintner's Plaza. The rain starts in. Visitors scramble for their cars as the downpour bungles their holiday.

Forward now, only forward.

Night Shot

"Listen to this, Nick. It says: Do not wear cologne, perfume, or any deodorants. No food of any kind is allowed, no bright clothing or flash cameras, and any women who are *menstruating* should please refrain from being on set while Jack is working. There will be a scaled-down crew for minimal distractions and safety reasons. Silence is imperative to Jack's performance . . ."

"He can smell women when they're . . . ?"

"I guess so. I wonder how they figured that out."

Cecil shifted his seat on the side fender of the livestock trailer and leaned forward on his knees to finish reading the call-sheet note to himself.

"We had a stud colt could smell my sister," Nick said, zipping up his jacket and walking the length of the truck and trailer, then turning and walking back. "Wooh!

Temperature dropped, huh?" He pulled his collar up around his neck and rubbed his skinny arms as he kept moving, clapping his hands together and pacing more deliberately.

Cecil read the last of the note and looked up at the scrubland of southeastern New Mexico. A table-rock jutted oddly in the distance, stretching a hard dark line along the last light from the horizon.

"He could smell her?" he asked, watching Nick walk in front of the line that faded off indefinitely from where the sun had set.

"Yeah, son of a bitch was a dog-gentle three-year-old, then, bam, just lost his nut when Treenie came into the round-pen one time. Got all studdy with his lip up, pawin', shakin' his head, rarin' up. Knocked her down! Lucky I was there – he coulda killed her."

"And she was havin' her period?"

"I don't know about that. I guess she was . . ."

"Well, that's what we're talkin' about Nick, isn't it?"

"All I know is he rared up on 'er. He sure didn't try to rare up on me!"

"Well, he knew you'd whoop his ass."

"He knew she was female is what it is. He knew she was . . . you know. You know what I mean."

Cecil leaned back against the cool aluminum side of the trailer and looked up at the few stars that were beginning to come through.

"See now," he said, "here I had this idea of your sister

floatin' in a cloud of high school and sweaters and little pink things, and now I'm seein' a bay horse mountin' her in a round-pen. I don't want that in my head, Nick."

"I didn't say he mounted her! Jesus."

"Well, that's the picture I get. I get a bay . . . Hell, maybe he just didn't like Treenie."

"No, he liked her plenty. Believe me."

They lit cigarettes and blew the smoke downward, looking off in separate directions – Cecil up at the sky and Nick out at the brush and boulders of the low ridge behind the truck and trailer, still rubbing his arms and pacing.

The ten horses they had hauled in earlier from Alamogordo were already on the Mexican camp set half a mile away, turned out in a small pen in the background. The camp was to be the focus of the night shot. Kelly, the gang boss, was there overseeing the simple positioning of the horses, the only concern being the structural integrity of the fake corral. He had fed them, and they were settled in. Cecil, Nick, and Kelly all knew the horses would likely never be seen in the shot, but there was always a chance of the camera panning over to them. They would have to remain on standby through the night unless, by some stroke of luck, the first AD released them early.

"A little deductive reasoning, and a guy could figure which women were havin' their period, huh, Nick?"

"What? Yeah, I reckon."

"I mean, if your little focus-puller gal, what's her name, Cleo? . . ."

"Chloe," Nick corrected him.

"Chloe. If she ain't on set when old Jack comes out – "

"No, I get it. I get it," Nick cut in.

"Here they come," Cecil said, suddenly serious, pointing toward the horizon.

The twelve-mile dirt road from the highway to base camp had been invisible in the twilight until a long procession of crew vehicles appeared near the base of the table-rock mesa. The headlights broke through in a bright line, fading back in the dust stirred up by the wheels. Cecil stood and walked alongside Nick to the front of the trailer for a better view of the crew cars boiling through the sand and dirt toward them.

"I hate night work," Nick said, standing transfixed by the nearing lights.

"Yeah. Me too."

Cecil and Nick could have been the same man from the back in their old beaver-felt hats. Their thinness and height were identical and equally extreme – no one could ever get their names straight. They reflected each other's manner in every movement, functioning with a lean toward work that suggested a belief in better things down the road.

"So what scene is it tonight?" Nick asked, breaking out of his headlight trance and turning to Cecil.

"What?"

"What scene are they shooting?"

"It's another camp deal. The Mexicans are camping again, I guess, and then Jack comes in and tears shit up."

Nick looked back to the oncoming cars. "We're not gonna have the *horses* down there when he's tearin' shit up, are we?"

"No, 'course not."

Nick paused before he spoke, his eyes still drawn to the vans and trucks that were within half a mile of them now.

"So why do we even have them here tonight? I mean, they ain't gonna see 'em anyway, but if they got Jack tearin' shit up, they know for damn sure we ain't gonna have any freakin' horses on the set with him, right?"

"Well, yeah. They know that."

"That's predator and prey! Am I right? I mean they don't expect . . ."

"You're right, Nick. Don't get bent up, it ain't gonna happen."

"So why are we even here? If they know that, why are we . . ."

"Come on, you know the deal. They've got to do their 'establishing' shot of the camp or whatever, set the scene. Maybe they'll see the horses in the background, maybe not, who knows. When Jack comes on, we'll be long gone. They can put the whole thing together later. We might even get outta here early."

The vans and equipment roared by without slowing –

camera crew, extras, stake-bed trucks, and rental cars – billowing a wall of sand and dust engulfing the two men. They ducked and ran to their truck, slamming the doors shut once inside.

"Assholes," Nick said from the passenger side. "You'd think people would have a little more sense, you know?"

Cecil pointed quickly to a truck and trailer at the back of the train of cars. "There he is!"

Both men were silent. They watched through the windshield as a red pickup towing a small armored-steel box trailer with barred vent slits along the top edge passed in front of them. The mysterious cargo floated by through the dust, angling away toward base camp, bold red letters stenciled on the back gate: JACK KODIAK – KEEP BACK.

They remained silent for a spell.

"How big *is* that son of a bitch?" Nick asked.

Cecil dug in his pocket for the call-sheet note. "I think it said he was fifteen hundred pounds or something . . . let's see, it says Jack weighs *eighteen* hundred pounds . . ."

"Eighteen hundred!" Nick yelled.

"Yeah. Eighteen hundred pounds and stands eleven feet high on his hind legs. He is as fast as a man . . . Kodiaks are the largest breed of bear in the world . . . Well, you sure wouldn't want to rile him."

"No sir," Nick said.

"Now your sister ain't gonna be down there tonight, is she?"

"Shut up."

They both laughed and rolled down the windows an inch.

"Now why in hell would a Kodiak bear be in New Mexico?" Nick asked. "That's gotta be the dumbest thing I ever heard. Kodiak, ain't that in the Yukon or something? Alaska? Who would believe one of those fuckers was down here in this country? Answer me that."

"It's a movie, Nick. They're making a movie."

"I know that. That's exactly what's wrong with the whole deal. You got to believe in it, right? Isn't the whole point to make something you can believe, make it seem possible? I mean, they might as well have a goddamn *moose* walk into camp, or hell, you want a bear, make him a polar bear for Christ's sake . . . I don't want to be connected to any movie that's got Kodiak bears and *Mexicans* in the same shot. That's just dumb."

"You're not connected to it, Nick."

"What do you mean, I'm not connected to it?"

"Nobody gives a shit about our horses. You think they care that we've been workin' sixteen-hour days and feedin' and haulin' and eatin' dust and all that? 'Course not. This ain't about horses, Nick."

Both men sat still while the dust cleared. They waited for several minutes without speaking until the lights from base camp came on – cutting clean into the air as the generators rumbled alive with little spouts of diesel smoke, and the remote patch of desert was illuminated with spears of work lights.

"We better go check on Kelly," Cecil said. "They're gearing up down there."

They stepped out into the chill and began walking the washboard road toward the set. The Condor crane was booming its basket from the base of the low ridge, the thirty-thousand-watt light breaking across the expanse of desert, reflecting off the natural amphitheater walls that surrounded the set. The crane climbed steadily, resounding eerie hydraulic noises and casting harsh unfiltered light over the brush and sparse mesquite until gaining its maximum height of fifty feet, where it stopped, swaying slightly from the halt.

The two men tilted their heads down, shading their eyes from the Condor with the brims of their hats, and walked toward the lights and bustle of base camp. Semitrailers, parked on either side of the road, created a canyon corridor leading to the catering tent that peaked in silhouette ahead of them. Shadowed people worked in the trailers, loading equipment on carts, calling to each other in jargon specific to their departments: electric, grips, camera, props. Crews lowered sandbags and light stands, bounce boards, apple boxes. Static radio voices filled walkie-talkies with excessive confirmations and reconfirmations, crackling like fighter pilots over the whine of liftgates and four-wheel-drive Kawasakis carting cables and gear down to the set.

Nick stopped when they reached the tent, rubbing his arms again.

"You want a cup of coffee? I'm freezin' my ass off here."

"Yeah. Grab Kelly one, too. I'll meet you at the set."

Nick ducked off toward the catering truck, and Cecil continued on, following the power cables on the ground that channeled juice to the set. The cables traced the perimeter of the tent and cut down an already worn path in the sand, sloping between the sage and scrub, giving deep under Cecil's feet in the darkness. He passed a young production assistant talking seriously into a headset as he hurried back to base. Cecil chuckled at him and walked on into the no-man's-land separating the work lights of the crew staging area from the warm amber-gel lights of the set. He could see greensmen and set dressers working quietly as he closed the forty-yard distance, the din of the crew fading behind him.

Rows of tan canvas tents, spread out in a massive Mexican Army camp, lined a clearing from the base of the rock ridge down to the edge of the brush. Cedar support stakes and eighteen-hundreds pots and utensils were laid alongside stone-circled fire pits, with saddles, rifles, and bedrolls piled up by the makeshift corral that held the ten horses.

Cecil stepped into the clear by the camera cart and stood for a moment, soaking up the stillness before cast and crew moved in. Even in the artificial light, the scene had the life of another time. Cecil thought it had to be the land that made the camp seem real and the modern equipment look so foreign. The difference struck him as somewhat profound, the made-up world in the real world. He stood with the thought, looking at the calm set until Kelly yelled from behind the corral.

"Cecil! Get over here!"

The horses swung their heads up from eating and shuffled against the rails of the cramped pen, tensing from the volume of the man's voice.

"Hey! Quit!" Kelly yelled at them.

Cecil jogged over, seeing the horses mash together.

"What's wrong?" he asked, reaching the pen.

Kelly stepped into the light, his torso thick and hard as a wrecking ball. "What's wrong? I've been trying to call you on the radio for twenty fuckin' minutes to get you down here! We gotta get the horses off the set 'cause the goddamned bear is workin' first! Is your radio on?"

"I don't have the radio," Cecil said.

"Where the hell is it? Where the fuck's Nick?"

"He's getting coffee . . ."

"Coffee! We got to pull the horses out. They're waitin' on us here!"

"All right."

"This piece-of-shit pen couldn't hold a dead goat. They'd all been runnin' loose if I'd a left . . . Where the fuck is

Nick, goddamn it! You got me lookin' like a moron here – screamin' at a radio and they're waitin' on us!"

"I'm sorry."

Cecil fell in immediately to halter the horses. He moved quickly, slipping through the rails with an armload of halters, talking softly to settle the geldings.

"Where's the bear now?" he asked, leading two horses out the gate and handing the ropes to Kelly.

"He's in his trailer at base camp. They're gonna try and pull the rig down closer to set once we're gone."

Kelly circled the horses behind him, waiting while Cecil haltered the others and handed him the ropes, leading them out one and two at a time until all ten were outside milling in a tethered mob around the two men.

The horses blew nervous warning snorts through their nostrils, and looked toward the lights of base camp, their ears alert, white showing in the edges of their eyes.

"They can smell him, I think," Cecil said, draping a lead rope over the neck of Zeke, the quietest horse of the group, and tying the loose end back to the halter to make reins.

He swung up on Zeke's bare back and gathered four of the ropes from Kelly, lining out the horses he was leading on either side.

"Just head to the trailer. I'll send Nick with the rest," Kelly told him.

"Aren't you comin'?"

"No, I got to talk to the first assistant."

"All right . . . Come on, boys."

Cecil squeezed Zeke's sides with his heels and clucked to the four others, hitting a jig away from set toward the brush.

Nick had scalded himself several times trying to balance three paper cups of coffee, holding them in a triangle ahead of him. He stumbled through the deep sand toward the edge of the brush as Cecil jogged up to him bareback with his five horses abreast.

"What's goin' on?"

"Don't say anything, just grab the rest of the horses and get 'em off the set!"

"What happened?"

"That bear's workin' first, and they're waitin' on us."

Cecil's lead horses sidestepped from the holdup, and he yanked the outside ropes to get them back in line.

"We're takin' 'em back to the trailer?" Nick asked.

"Yeah, come on! Kelly's hot. I wouldn't say nothing, just get 'em off the set."

Cecil clucked again, and the five horses leapt into a trot.

"You want your coffee?" Nick called after him.

"You're better off ridin' Parson – he don't lead for shit," Cecil yelled over his shoulder. "And keep Buddy on your right, you know how he is."

"Oh, great, leave Parson and Buddy for me. I get it."

Cecil jogged off through the dark sand and juniper, the

Condor light catching the top of his hat and the slick backs of the horses.

"Nick!" Kelly screamed. "Get your ass over here!"

"Yes, sir."

He burned himself again with the coffee and cursed as he hurried up to Kelly and the five remaining horses.

"I brought you some coffee."

"I don't want any fuckin' coffee – just get these god-damned horses outta here!"

Nick turned in a circle, still holding the cups, trying to find a place to set them down.

"Goddamn it, Nick!"

"Oh, hell," Nick said, dropping the cups on the ground.

The horses shifted anxiously from the tension in the men's voices, the foreign smells, and the hard shadows thrown by the disorienting lights. They pitched and set back on the ropes, clearing their bowels and calling to the five others that had left with Cecil.

"Give me Parson."

Nick ducked under two of the ropes Kelly held that were stretched tight to Hammer and Buddy.

"Whoa, you son of a bitch!" Kelly yelled at them as Nick worked through the tangle of ropes, grabbing Parson's lead and tying it back to the halter.

"I reckon they can smell old Jack out there," Nick said, swinging onto the sorrel's back and scooting forward to his withers.

"They're gonna smell a lot of him if you don't get movin'!" Kelly barked, handing him the rest of the lead ropes.

The headlights of the red truck panned into view, bouncing across the tents with the steel box trailer twisting behind it.

"I need Buddy on my right!" Nick yelled, seeing the truck. He scrambled to organize the ropes in his free hand, flipping them behind his back and pulling on the animals' heads as they swung their hard necks and tried to start off in the direction of the other horses. He cursed and jerked, yelling their names as he untangled the ropes.

"Damn it, Chili, Jet – get over here!"

He maneuvered Parson between the four lead horses and allowed their impulse to follow the others to take over, hitting a long trot after Cecil, who was already at the base camp road.

"This could get Western," Nick said to himself, hearing the four-wheel-drive gears of the red truck behind him laboring toward the set.

The horses grew strong in his hand, pulling ahead of Parson, jumping the brush and diving through the uneven sand that spread black ahead of them. Nick gripped with his calves and braced against the ropes in his right hand, feeling the power of the five horses gain momentum and surge head-to-head across the ground. The work lights hit only high points of the scrub brush, giving the illusion of pits and chasms in the shadows. Nick pulled back, trying to slow the horses, but being bareback with only halters, he was at a disadvantage. They grew stronger, loping across the black brush. He moved parallel to the tent on his right, passing base camp and the semis parked along the road. He could see the silver roof of the horse trailer in the distance, farther than he thought, the terrain reversed and strange. His right hand clenching the ropes throbbed, and he squeezed his knees in, sitting deep into Parson's back. The horses grew stronger, Hammer and Jet pulling on the outside, spread wide across a flat stretch dodging brush, then mashed back together like bellows, crushing Buddy and Chili against Nick's legs. He spurred Parson to keep up with the others, feeling his control slip as all five accelerated. The power switched to the animals, the inherent fear that made them creatures of flight propelling the herd to escape a foreign danger, a scent, a hint of the unknown in the dark and sounds. Nick was a passenger, relying on his ability to move with them. He let them roll. He stopped fighting and let them run hard, grabbing hold of Parson's mane and clinging to his back as the five flattened out and flew across the ground, their heads lunging in a wild tempo, charging competitively. Tears streamed back to his ears as his hat blew off and caught up on the stampede string around his neck, flapping behind his head. He could see the horse trailer, the safety of the trailer, the stopping point. The horses jumped the brush at the road edge together, catching more speed in the flat. Their feet rumbled loud, pounding the hard-packed dirt, stirring dust and throwing crazy shadows in front of them.

Cecil had finished tying the last of his five horses to the trailer when they heard the sound on the road and swung their rear ends away to face the incoming roar head-on. They craned their necks and set back on the ropes.

"Ho, now!" Cecil yelled at them, trying to see down the road. He raised his hand to cover the Condor that shone in his eyes and saw dust swirling into the high lights. The backlit mass of the running horses appeared, bearing down on the trailer with Nick's thin silhouette perched in the middle. They covered the space in four strides, bringing the dust, and sat back on their hocks sliding up to the trailer and the tied horses, knocking their heads together and colliding with the others, blowing snot and heaving.

"What the hell!" Cecil yelled. "Whoa now, whoa!"

Nick slipped off to his feet and dropped the ropes, stepping clear of the mix of horses and hunched over to catch his air.

"See now," he said, pulling his hat back on, "they shoulda had a camera rollin' on *that*!"

Cecil grabbed the loose horses and pulled them away from the others.

"You get run off with?" He laughed.

"I'll say. They had my ass comin' across there!"

"I thought maybe old Jack was chasin' ya!"

"Yeah, I think they thought he was too," Nick said, still winded, shaking the pain out of his right hand.

They led the runaways to the other side of the trailer and tied them equal distance apart, speaking in reassuring tones to settle the group.

"Don't tell Kelly, now," Nick said. "I mean, nobody's hurt or nothin'."

"He's just gonna laugh," Cecil said, laughing himself.

"Come on, I don't need that."

The animals' breath steamed in the cold air, clouding around their long heads as the two men looked them over. They quieted, slowly relaxing as the structure of the herd was restored.

"I guess we just have to wait now," Cecil said, pulling his cigarettes from his chest pocket and flipping one part way out of the pack for Nick. "You were hookin' it pretty good there, Nick. You all right?"

"Yeah."

"Too bad your little Cleo gal didn't see you comin' across there like Powder River . . ."

"*Chloe.*"

"Cowboy that you *are,* you woulda been snortin' her flank for sure if she'd seen that."

"Oh, hell."

Nick and Cecil climbed back into the truck and everything went quiet again. They blew smoke out their windows, looking into the tall door mirrors at the dim reflection
of the horses tied to the trailer behind them, and then out
the windshield to the lights in the distance.

"Who's this?" Nick said, pointing to a figure in the road
coming toward them. The young assistant that Cecil had
passed at base camp walked up to the truck looking in
on them.

"Didn't we issue you guys a radio? Where's your radio?"
he asked, walking around to Nick's window. "Your boss
is pretty perturbed, he's walking back now. Copy that!"
He yelled into his mouthpiece, holding the walkie-talkie
up in his hand like a liberty torch. "I'll relay . . . You're
released . . . No horses work in shot. Copy . . . Did you
hear that?" he said.

"Who are you talking to?" Cecil asked.

"You! You guys are wrapped. You can 'load 'em up' or
whatever you do."

"We're wrapped?" Nick asked.

"Yes! You. Are. Released. Go home. Good night!"

"No shit?"

The assistant turned and walked back toward base camp.

"Can you believe that?" Nick said.

"I know. What a little prick."

"No, I mean them bringing us all the way out here for
nothing. What a bunch of crap."

"Well, I ain't gonna argue with 'em."

They got back out of the truck and walked down either side of the trailer, passing behind the dark horses. They reached the back and unlatched the double doors.

"I kinda wanted to see Jack work, though," Cecil said, swinging his side open.

"I came about as close as I want, I think."

They laughed and untied the first two horses. They knew the order to put them on the trailer without having to discuss it, and they quietly loaded them for the ride back home.

In the Open

Will was more than an hour into the state park, but he hadn't stopped to hide yet. The morning was pale, full of birds, squirrels, insect noises. The coastal fog still dampened the acoustics in the bay and oak trees as he crunched dust from the dry leaves that covered the ground. He hiked the slight slope, focusing on the immediate obstacles of logs and brush without raising his eyes to take in the vast acreage that rolled around him, diving in soft California draws toward Mendocino County and the Pacific.

The sounds oddly reminded him of the early mornings at home when he was awake before anyone – the whirs and gurgles of self-timed suburban sprinklers, the ambient hum of street cleaners working their dung-beetle pace, the calming mesh of domestic bird life and yard noise that settled on the neighborhood before the people ventured out and the cars and leaf blowers swept it all to a heartless wash. The peace of the park consumed him and he hiked with deliberation, comparing the personal calm of his accustomed sensations to the rich musk and dirty honey-fragrance of the vegetation around him. He felt he could travel in it forever, in the solitude, that it was in the state of smelling and listening and taking in the newborn gift of the day that a rare appreciation of what was always below the din of the world arose in him.

"How was work?" he knew he'd said to Steph, as he always did when she came in. She dropped layers of clothes on several surfaces throughout the house, her briefcase and keys on the couch.

"The same. You know." She walked out of her shoes, leaving them frozen in the span of her regular step. She pressed the playback button on the answering machine and continued barefoot to the bedroom and adjoining bathroom to shower. Will could picture it now as he hiked – the darkness outside the windows that saddened the house, the night version of the house that hid from the sunlit rooms in the day, enclosed with no sense of the yard, the street, the trees. He thought it a shame that the house should be abandoned every morning at its brightest, that it was only inhabited in the evenings and long nights before they both went to work.

"Why are you looking at me like that?" Steph had said, shaking her fingers in her hair to speed the drying time.

"What do you mean?"

She let it go, moving toward the basic pasta and salad dinner he had prepared on the cutting-block island in the kitchen.

"Oh, you've outdone yourself, William."

She sneaked a bell-pepper sliver and smiled, snapping the freshness in her teeth. He felt he was off the hook, that she approved of his unsaid actions with her playful glance.

He hadn't told her that he'd been switched to part-time at the Land Management building. He knew it wouldn't go well, so he'd put it off for a week. She wouldn't find the same relief *he* found in working fewer hours.

She kissed his cheek and gathered the salad bowl and bread. He wiped his hands on the dish towel and joined her at the dinner table with the pasta.

"I thought of you today," he had said, still lifted by her appreciation of his meal and the relief in her easy way. He hoped the statement might linger in the room on its own, that it summed up his good feeling as it was.

"What did you think?"

He wanted to tell her about his work then. That was the time.

"I thought maybe we should get a dog, a puppy," he said.

She stopped chewing.

He could see her forehead grow cool above her dark eyes, and he dreaded her response. He regretted saying it;

it wasn't what he wanted to say. The puppy could have been an idea, but he wanted to be up front with her; he wanted to feel closer.

"So where was the thought of me?" she said.

"It's just an idea . . ."

"You need to think these things through, Will."

He tried to return her in his head to the smile and glance in the kitchen, tried to retain the kiss on the cheek as something close. He didn't speak, reasoning that a silence might hold more weight than anything he could say.

The fog was burning off in the park now, but Will still hadn't stopped to hide. He was preoccupied, marching into new territory. Broken thoughts slipped through – the cool temperature holding his scent close to the ground. Man's scent. Dogs. Olfactory receptor cells – five million in humans, two hundred twenty million in dogs. He thought the numbers were right – they were in his head from somewhere.

He could picture Steph as he undid the neck and chest buttons of his coat to release the heat he'd built up from hiking. He thought of their talks that ultimately resulted in silences, the testy bathroom procedures where they were forced to occupy the same space, the bed where he pretended to sleep while she lay hard as bone in the dark beside him. He could see her in her late-for-work frenzy, searching for all the belongings she had randomly spread across the house the night before, her indignation building to a fury by the time she went out the door. He could see her perfectly in all her movements, and he missed her. Even envisioning her angry, he missed her. He wished she could know he was missing her. He wished she could see him in the trees.

His decision to volunteer was so impulsive after being cut back at work, such a departure from his pedestrian ten-key office job, that he kept it a secret. He feared "volunteer work" would sound contrived to Steph, that she would suspect him of having an affair or something, so he decided not to tell her. He hadn't known exactly what he was getting into when he volunteered; volunteering for anything was something new. He had assumed it would be mundane chores like cleaning out kennel runs or doing flea dips, fund-raising maybe. But any of those tasks would be welcome, and the words "search and rescue" alone excited him, even if it was to be less romantic than it sounded.

The initial seminar had been held in the parking lot at the base of the state park. The head of the program, a short homely woman in a khaki jumpsuit and green cap, had gone over the principles and safety precautions while pacing in front of ten beige plastic crates that held all the young dogs. The dogs watched her steps through the door grills as she handed out pamphlets and releases to be signed by the six volunteers. Will didn't know any of the other people and didn't plan to partake in the free lunch that followed the morning meeting. He still had his afternoon shift at work.

"This is not a game," the head trainer had said, making eye contact with those closest to her. "I expect each of you to take it seriously, and I will say it again, *please* do not play with the puppies unless specifically asked to do so by the individual trainers that you will each be coupled with. These are working, professional dogs. They are not pets! So I will reiterate: Unless you are told to praise the animals, please refrain from handling them. When we get out in the field, situations will arise where you will need to praise, but we will show you then how to praise correctly."

Will realized then that he and the others were providing themselves as bait for the dogs in training. "Dummy runs," she called it, which stirred a chittering laugh through the five other volunteers. Will was thrilled that his only duty lay in hiking out alone into the state park and hiding. The rest of the responsibility was on the dogs and trainers to track and find him.

He'd been out twice since the seminar, pretending to be stranded in the park. He knew two of the eight-month-old German shepherd dogs now, Betsy and Lily, as well as their hip-heavy trainer, Linda, who seemed to have a personality only when she was talking to the puppies.

His first time out, he settled in a dry runoff ditch after hiking for nearly an hour. He hadn't known how long he'd have to wait, so he chose the easy cradling slant of the ditch feeling sure he could hold out in that position for hours if necessary.

Lily found him in fifteen minutes.

His second run took longer, hiking farther into the park for Betsy. He found a hideout under the arch of an oak tree that had fallen to a downslope, where he covered himself in leaves and waited.

Betsy found him in half an hour.

Both times Will was found, he praised the pups madly as he'd been instructed, waiting alone with each salivating one until Linda showed up and did the official praising. Will knew he would never be able to match Linda's sickening pitch of jubilation that put the dogs beside themselves, pissing happy. But he did his best.

The fog was gone now, and the late-morning sun came clean through the branches as Will continued into the thicker heart of the park. He forgot the limit of the training range, the principle of stopping after an hour. Linda had gone over it all, explaining that Betsy would eventually graduate to longer and more demanding hunts, but for now she needed optimal conditions to hold her attention. She could lose interest if she wasn't rewarded within a certain radius.

All of this had slipped Will's mind as he hiked on; even his fascination with the cool weather holding his scent close to the ground had left him.

"How was work?" he said as he walked, picturing Steph hit the playback button and step out of her shoes.

"Don't ask," she answered, disappearing into the bedroom.

It was chicken night; he flipped breaded boneless pieces in a skillet, then dumped a brick of frozen corn into boiling water. He could barely hear the answering machine relaying women's voices in the living room, the same voices that were always sorry for missing Steph.

"How was work!" he had yelled from the kitchen, knowing she couldn't hear him.

The shower was running. He heard the Plexiglas door smack shut after she stepped in. He turned the hot water on full force in the sink, letting it run down the drain until he heard her shriek. Then he turned it off.

"Were you running the water while I was in the shower?" she said at the table.

"No."

"Did you hear me? I screamed!" she said, pausing with a forkful of chicken.

"No."

"You didn't hear me?"

"No."

"The shower went cold as ice!"

He continued eating.

"How was work?" he said.

"What?"

46

"How . . . was . . . work?"

"You know how it is. Why do you even ask? You know!"

She pushed the plate away and sat back.

"Why don't you call those women?" he said, and took a bite.

"What?"

"Those women on the machine."

"What're you talking about, what women?"

He pushed his plate away, too. He wanted to confront her. He wanted to tell her everything then.

"Are you keeping something from me?" she asked.

He cleared the table and carried everything back to the sink.

The silence came again – the silence that filled him. She had no idea where he was, he thought. She could never guess he was in the open. She would never hear his feet in the leaves.

Will suddenly remembered the dog. He stopped walking and sat down, the halt bringing his senses to the immediate surroundings. He checked his wristwatch, but he couldn't recall when he'd started off into the park. It had to have been more than an hour, he thought. The dog was on her way, he was sure.

He faced the direction he had come from and waited, feeling the spiky oak leaves jab through his pants and socks.

He shifted his ankles underneath him and sat Indian style, his range of vision limited to oak trunks, madrone, and manzanita. He could smell bay and eucalyptus. He could hear his watch. He closed his eyes and imagined little Betsy sniffing after his scent, her happy trot, the trainer behind giving encouragement. He smiled at the thought of the young dog whose sole purpose was to seek him out, her focused talent that would come undone once she found him. He would embrace her, he would hold her right up close, the soft ebullient creature that she was, the innocent simplicity of her nature beneath the influence and training of her master. He wanted to help her. He was impatient and he opened his eyes, straining to hear any sound of her coming toward him. He wanted to call out, but it was his job to stay quiet, his duty to hide even as it was unbearable.

Steph was in the shower when Will walked in the front door from his afternoon shift at work. He set his briefcase down next to hers on the couch and walked into the bedroom.

Darkness was coming earlier, and the pale lights of the high school football field glowed above the neighboring roofs. He looked out at the lights from the bedroom window, listening to the shower behind him. He remembered the smell of Bermuda grass when he was on the team in high school, the green-yellow lights, the bulkiness of his uniform. He had waited for the left guard to be injured, but he never was, so Will had sat on the side waiting, watching the bleacher mothers stand and hold their faces every time their boys hit the ground.

Will turned from the window and stood at the bathroom door, the heat of the rushing water rising through the lit gap at the bottom. He pictured Steph beyond it, scrubbing her body as if sanding a deck. He opened the door and stepped into the white light and steam.

"I'm in here!" Steph called out, her voice bouncing off the linoleum.

Will popped the Plexiglas door open from its magnet-latch and stepped, fully clothed, into the shower with her. The instant warmth of the water hit his collar and back, seeping into his coat with a comforting weight as the door clicked shut. He watched her back away to the end of the tub, disbelief filling her face as she scrambled to cover herself with her hands.

"I went too far," Will said, not moving from his position under the nozzle. "I called out . . . I retraced my steps to get within her range, but I'd gone too far. They found her back at the beginning trying to start again. She wanted to find me, she kept trying, but there wasn't enough to go on. They had to call her off . . . They had to stop her before she lost heart."

Will's clothes retained the water, and the drain went quiet – the spatter against his back the only sound. He watched Steph, motionless, clutching herself. He felt a relief in being so close.

Flaw in the Shelter

Rain fell the first day of September, causing panic for the vineyard managers, but the land only soaked it up in welcome calm. Carl found the quiet fulfilling, no longer a grape worker affected by the wine-industry concerns: mold, sugar count, frost. He saw a truth in nature, tamped into the stillness by the settling rain out his window – the valley oaks twisting in the morning grayness, frozen in their march across the leaning yellow pasture. He imagined the impossible life of roots beneath, tried to see the giant trees as they lived out their time in the same place, sometimes hoping they might hike up their skirts and scamper through the field while he wasn't looking.

Carl had already fed the horses and milked the goat, his small terrier trotting next to him through the morning routine. The animals welcomed the rain as well, blinking softly in eating bliss as the moisture beaded on their backs. He liked to watch the horses eat, the sanctity in their fixated chewing, their simple happiness.

He thought he'd make a fire, the first of the season, just to burn the cobwebs out of the stovepipe and cut the chill. The turn in weather made his shoulder ache. He'd never wanted to be an old man who predicted the weather by his arthritic conditions, but he was finding that to be the case. The cause of the injury was no longer of interest, it was the ache that he related to now.

He gathered wood from his shed that he'd already stocked for winter, only a hamperful and some kindling, not needing to jump headlong into winter preparation by filling the wood box outside his front door. It was only the first rain of the season.

He tried to remember the last fire he'd lit in the small freestanding stove, looking for a clue in the old ashes that covered the bottom. He didn't recognize anything in the charred bits and lit a twisted paper bag, shoving the flame up inside the stovepipe to warm the flue.

A sudden flit sounded within the pipe, startling him. He pulled his hand out, scraping his forearm against the edge of the door, and listened. The flutter again beat itself against the pipe up above the ceiling line, and his dog trotted over from the kitchen, peering keenly at the exciting rustle above their heads.

There had been bats in the attic the previous winter that

Carl had eradicated with an old bee smoker, puffing cool bay-leaf smoke into the crevices of the A-frame roof. He remembered watching the thick-bodied creatures slither out and cling to the exterior walls, trembling like little angry demons before he sealed the holes to the attic and left them to find a new home elsewhere.

But the flutter in the stovepipe was not a bat; he could hear the difference. It was a bird trapped inside, certainly feathers beating against the black metal cylinder and not clawed, leather wings.

Carl mashed the burning paper out on the bottom of the stove and considered the problem. There wasn't enough space through the narrow flue to allow the bird to free itself into the stove. That scenario would put the bird inside the house anyway. He figured he had to get it out through the top, but obviously the bird had trouble flying up and out of the chimney.

These were the situations that Carl often found himself in, unforeseen events that hindered a natural momentum through his day. Seeing a broken water line or a fallen oak tree, an injured or trapped animal – whether it was the horses or the goat or the neighbor's cow – *that* became the duty and purpose of his day. He really didn't mind having to tend to the things that gave a certain structure to his time on the property. Now that he was no longer a grape worker and merely a caretaker of a lazy nonworking ranch, the chores that broke away from the usual mundane maintenance were almost uplifting. But it seemed to him these hindrances were happening more frequently, and this morning he really only wanted to relax in the change of season and have a peaceful fire.

The wings flapped madly within the pipe again, and he knew the problem would not fix itself.

The rain had subsided, and a cold gray dampness pressed in, spitting occasional droplets. He put his coat on and ventured out to get his ladder.

His toolshed seemed oddly small and dark in the wetness, the rain giving the usually proud sun-baked structure a demure and shriveled humility. Everything was changed by the rain, he felt, walking back with the ladder over his shoulder. Even his farmhouse seemed to shrink from the moisture, whereas the pink hydrangeas surrounding his wooden deck and bedroom window looked vibrant, expanding in the rich saturation.

The smell was different, the freshness. He'd heard something once of positive and negative ions, he couldn't place where he'd heard it, but the rain supposedly released one of the two, and wind produced the other. He didn't know which was which. He knew he hated the wind, and so did the animals. It stirred everything up to a maddening and unsettling pitch of dust and gusts that jaded him and made him short-tempered. He knew he loathed the wind and enjoyed the rain, and he'd rather not break it down to a scientific explanation. Everything these days seemed to be broken down or made easier or made terribly clear in order to give a person yet another thing to worry about. That's why he didn't read the news. It was better not to be made guilty for one's lack of action, to not be partnered with the droves who were more concerned with what's happening in Indonesia, or God knows where, than their own backyard. It made sense to him to allow the rest of the planet to follow its own course and for him to follow his. What can you do for people in Indonesia that you can't do for your neighbors across the creek? That was something Carl found himself thinking whenever the topic of world status came into his head. Like the time he came home from the feed store and the neighbors' Holstein cow had gotten a gate stuck around her head. It was a small gate, one that might pass a man, with an opening in the middle. Apparently the cow had poked her nose through the center to graze on the other side and when she picked her head up she lifted the gate off the hinges, lodging it behind her ears to frame her black and white head. She had inadvertently opened the gateway as a result and then wandered onto Carl's property to graze and ruminate. Carl had devoted most of the day to removing the gate from the old Holstein's neck. The neighbors were, of course, not at home, and he'd had to throw a rope over the gentle cow's head and tie her to a tree to pull it off. But it was that sort of situation that he could relate to, that he could see jumping to arms and rectifying. Immediacy was the only thing at hand, the only thing worth recognizing as truth.

Carl leaned the ladder against the drain gutter and climbed up the rungs. He didn't have a plan other than pulling the small chimney pipe out of the roof and hoping the bird flew free – it seemed like a situation that might define itself as it went.

The roof was wet, the hard slanting angle of shingles slick and mossy from the constant shade of the enormous live oak that struck out above it. He wondered if he might have more traction barefoot, but he tried his boots on the surface, leaning tentative weight as if it were a frozen pond. Finding the grip satisfactory, he climbed from the last unsafe ladder step.

Maybe people don't have enough in their day, Carl thought, mincing open-armed like a mummy for the chimney far up on the incline. If there was substance and reason within their work and function, they might see the unimportance of Indonesia, they might see the futility of venturing their interests away from their realm. It used to be that there was enough titillation within people's immediate surroundings that life sustained itself, that it held enough weight to keep it on the ground and not flip into lofty delusions of world peace that distract people from their duty to the land in front of them.

He grabbed hold of the chimney and hung on like a novice roller skater to a traffic light, the slickness of the roof more treacherous near the apex of his house.

The high vantage point was new to him, seeing the

horses in the pasture below, facing in the same direction, their heads down. He could see the goat in her little pen beside them, the neighbors' cow across the way, the vineyards beyond glowing green in the distance. The new perspective filled him with a strange hope, a hope of still being able to see things for the first time. The moments of first sight seemed long gone – nothing had been new to him for many years, he thought. He missed those moments: coming to this property for the first time or walking into a vineyard as nothing more than a kid thirty years ago. His expectations at the time had been different, his impulse had been to back away and search for other work, work that might have had more potential, more reward. He'd had a fear of being trapped, of belonging to something, a class maybe. But having pushed through initial unfamiliarity, he'd found a purpose that he'd always hoped for. The grape work was good; there was value in the labor. He matured with it and found reward in the simplicity. The same went for his caretaking job. It was a new chapter in his life, an acceptance of his age and place, having earned the nobility to give a patron peace of mind.

The bird's panic echoed in the chimney, bouncing off the gripless walls.

Carl hugged the pipe to his belly and hoisted upward, raising it a foot but not clearing it from the roofline. He squatted down and hoisted again, raising it another foot but still not pulling it free of the house. His feet slipped, and he leaned in against the pipe to regain his balance, tilting it at an awkward angle. He pulled again and uncorked the hole, pulling the six-foot piece of pipe free. He teetered with the unwieldy thing for a moment before setting the bottom edge on the shingles, then carefully he laid it down on the slant. He took a few breaths, looking down to the hard angle that dropped away toward the gutters and then the twelve-foot drop to the ground. It would be a waste to fall, he thought, an unsung act of heroism for an ignorant bird. He steadied himself, regaining his footing, and peered down the open hole. The strange angle from above looking down the dark tube into his attic unnerved him, the vulnerability of the roof maybe, the open gap to the elements. He felt disoriented, looking through the flaw in the shelter. The bird was no longer of interest, not seeing or hearing the mad flaps, only a darkness and silence within the pipe, unlit and exposed beneath him.

The quiet confused him now, the sudden still detachment from the original purpose. He lifted his head and breathed in the cool humidity. Everything was behind him, he felt, all the years, the harvests, the fruit he'd reaped like a machine. That was all behind him, and just like his shoulder, dislocating it from a fall off a grape truck and working with his arm strapped across his torso for a month, that time was gone. He only had the tale and the ache now. He was alone with it, with everything that had led through his days to mounting his roof and pulling the chimney pipe out like a stubborn arrow from a boar, seeing its heart in the cavity – seeing the core that's hidden behind hide its entire life.

Carl's feet gave way with the velocity of a scythe cutting wheat. Felled by gravity, he slapped backward, cracking his head with the full swing of weightlessness. Stunned by the ungiving wood of the roof, he slid feetfirst on his back to the edge, catching his heels in the rain gutter where he stopped.

He lay still on the slant, his knees bent, his feet holding him at the edge. He rested, feeling his worried heartbeat through his skull and neck, the cool damp shingles at his back. He looked over his forehead at the roofline behind and above him, a strange dark horizon against the gray clouds. He could hear his dog in the hydrangeas below, whining at the ladder. He knew the horses would still be eating, the goat would be belching cud.

He lay still, and the rain started again, slapping cold pecks on his face. The live oak limbs fingered above him, as if submerged in a gray sea beneath him, spitting upward at him. He felt he could leap to the tree, that the roof held him to it, that he could let go into the quiet of the rain.

The small bird fluttered from the hole in the shingles and rested for a moment at the lip of the orifice. It shook the soot and cobwebs from its head and wings, then took flight, streaking a dull sparrow-brown arc. Carl saw its flight. He saw it resume its life, and a value became clear, a value he hadn't seen since he could remember.

Nurturer by Nature

"I get goose bumps thinkin' about it!"

I look at his arm catching the dash light of the El Camino, and I don't see any goose bumps.

"I really don't know which way it'll go, you know what I mean?"

"Yeah," I say. "I know what you mean."

Marco shouldn't be driving; there's no flow to his execution, drifting across the two-lane coast road and swerving through the dark.

"Look at that moon!" he says.

"*Don't* look at the moon," I tell him, seeing it big as a pancake over the Pacific, the headlands crumbling down to the shelf of Highway 1, then carrying on to the rocks and surf hundreds of feet below.

"So, she doesn't know then?" I say.

"What?"

"She doesn't know you're doing this."

"She'll eventually know. You'll tell her probably."

"Me?" I ask.

He looks at me across the dark cab, a look that lasts too long and makes him swerve back into the lane.

"Maybe I should drive, huh?"

"Relax. We're close, man. We're getting close."

The belligerent mystery in his voice worries me, a tone that makes the driving seem secondary – I know we'll make it, it's the arriving that's dangerous.

"You really shouldn't do this, Marco," I say, as if I don't know the story.

"That's right, Ricardo." He laughs. "I should not do this."

He's always called me Ricardo. "Marco and Ricardo" like dancing chipmunks or something. Never Richard, Dick, Richie, just Rich or Ricardo.

We turn down an impossibly steep driveway, one you'd need a system of funny-house mirrors and a running start to make it back onto the highway without getting creamed.

"Here, man," he says, handing me a bottle of sunblock from behind the seat.

"What's this?"

"Just put some on. Put it on your face."

"It's one in the morning!"

"They love Coppertone."

We descend the long driveway that hugs the cliff wall, winding through Monterey pines and brush toward the beach below.

"Coppertone?" I ask.

"That's what they're into. It's like an aphrodisiac with these two. Surfers . . . lifeguards . . . it transports them, I'm not kidding."

We pull up to a small beach house. Potted plants in macramé hangers, sand-dollar wind chimes, beaded found-art mobiles cluttering the porch.

"I don't think we should do this."

"What?"

"I shouldn't do this," I say.

"Of course you shouldn't, family man. This is the last thing you should do."

He steps out of the El Camino. The wind catches his coat as he pulls it on, flapping it across his back like a pissed-off flag, and he springs onto the deck and rings the doorbell. I wait in the car, listening to its cool-down noises while he stands at the door, his back to me, framed in silhouette by the obscured light humming through the opaque glass. I expect him to turn around with a devious look that I remember, a look from twenty years ago, but he faces the door – a new mature commitment to infidelity in his posture.

The door opens for him and a strange, humiliating queasiness slips in my gut.

A backlit female figure in a dark sarong freezes for a

moment beyond him. She clutches him in a hug, vanishing behind his body with only her hands visible around his neck. They don't kiss. She leads him inside then stares out at me in the car, a tough, suspicious breadth in her shoulders and stance. She turns to him between the light, her dark profile soft and round, hardly a nose. She speaks to him, but I can't hear her over the wind outside the sealed car. She swings the door shut.

The Coppertone bottle is still in my hand, abstract sailboats and bikinied women painted on it. I dig under the seat for the whiskey we were working on in town, Fighting Cock, just like we used to. I take a pull, looking at the house being blown over by the surf breeze, the moon floating right above. The harsh liquor throws my stomach into upheaval with blistering heartburn, swelling my tongue. I salivate and belch, knowing the situation is only going to get worse. I take another sip.

Marco discovered the notes in Sherrie's car a month ago. He was looking for the garage opener, but he found all the balled-up slips of paper with words on them, words like *Friday* or *parking lot*. Some of them were complete sentences, complete in their conviction − *You make me realize what's missing.* Sherrie had called it off long before the discovery. She'd made it clear that it was over.

She said to me, "Please, Richard, just spend some time with him. Have a night like you used to."

I knew she thought it would help. She thought I might

convince him of something, his bind maybe, his commitment. Trust was a word that bounced around like a BB in a boxcar.

I taste the salt and moisture as I step out of the El Camino, the wind ripping through the chimes and knickknacks on the porch and pressing on my face. I take the whiskey and the sunblock and walk around the side of the one-level house, stumbling through dark sand and ice plants to a trail leading down to the beach. The surf is close, the sound of it flying at me with the wind, the sky clear, the fog blown inland. I look back at the house, tripping over driftwood and an old fire pit as I near the water, seeing a few lights through the small windows but no sign of Marco or the women.

The air is different just at the thought of us cheating, the freshness shoulder high, blowing hard on me like a separate pulse. I pull my shoes off and walk to the water, the foam oozing up and washing cold across my feet. I dig my toes into the thick sand as the water recedes, and my mind empties out with the sensation until a woman's voice I've never heard suddenly calls behind me, fighting the wind.

"Ricardo!" she yells.

She couldn't know me. I turn back and see a woman closing in on me through the sand, not the woman who stared at me from the doorway, a taller, stronger woman, leaning against the rushing air and pale light.

"Ricardo," she says again.

"Yes?"

"I'm Carla, Mickey's friend. You're Marco's brother?"

"Yeah."

"They said you were sitting in the car. You weren't there, so I figured you came down here."

She's taller than me, maybe six feet, coarse dark hair swaying around her face.

"So you're checking on me?" I ask, trying to see the color of her eyes.

"I guess so." She laughs.

"I'm all right out here," I say.

"So am I. You want to walk?"

"I don't need you to comfort me or anything . . ."

"Don't worry."

"I don't need to be entertained."

"You Catholic, Ricardo?"

"What?"

"You a God-fearing man?"

"No. It's Richard. Call me Richard."

"You were raised with God?"

"What is this?"

"I'm just curious, *Richard*. Don't get in a tizzy."

"I don't get in tizzies."

"Then talk to me. I'm just talking."

We walk north on the beach, the ocean to our left. I take a sip of the whiskey and recap it, my hands full carrying my shoes, the bottle, the sunblock.

"We celebrated Christmas," I say, bracing against the liquor.

"How 'bout Easter?"

"We dyed eggs and that. Candy . . ."

"But you didn't go to Mass."

"No."

High wispy clouds cruise inland above our heads.

I hand her the bottle. She takes a long sip, then covers her mouth and shakes her head.

"My God, that's horrible. Is that your choice?"

"It's a tradition."

I look at our bare feet, sand clinging to our toes as we walk.

"He shouldn't do this," I say, feeling safe outside.

"Shouldn't do what?" she asks like a therapist, her voice lowering.

"*This,* this thing, this event!"

"Event?"

"You know what I'm talking about, come on."

"He's in pain, Richard. She can help. Mickey's a real nurturer, you know?"

"He's not in pain."

"How would you know?" she asks.

"I know *he's* not the one in pain."

She stops walking. I sense it's a test to see if I'll stop walking as well, not a legitimate emotional need. I continue to walk, even with the obligation to stand with her, to say something to her, some comfort to get her walking again, heavying my steps. I walk, hearing the waves, seeing the wet rocks and boulders shine white with the moon against the sand, the cliff rising dark and rough to my right. I should look back, I guess. I've reached the point of looking back to see her standing in the sand – a stranger waiting for something I'm supposed to say, some explanation, some duty to keep the natural laws of empathy running uneventfully.

I stop and turn around. She's steadfast, forty yards behind me, facing the ocean. I start walking back to her with all the good intentions of a high schooler trying to make amends with a girl I know nothing about.

"Look, Carla," I say, reaching her. "I don't really know what your role is in this. I don't really know what I'm supposed to do. It's unexplored territory . . ."

"I know the territory very well. He needs our help."

"Whose help, you and Mickey?"

"Yes."

"Say 'help' ten times fast."

"What?"

"It's a weird word, 'help.' It's like a foreign word."

She turns and starts walking back toward the house.

"See, it's not like that," I yell, following ten feet behind her. "Some nurturing aid is not what's needed. That's the last thing that's needed, Carla."

"These ideas you have of 'how it is' and 'what's needed' are completely baseless."

"Stop! Will you stop?"

"What?" she says, stopping and facing me.

"You think you've got some firsthand knowledge that I don't, some inside line?"

"You're drunk."

"Am I? Am I way off the page here?"

"You're stumbling around with your shoes in your hand, and what's that, sunblock? It's the middle of the night, you're wearing sunblock, preaching craziness about what's needed, and your brother, your blood, is – "

"I'm not *wearing* it."

"What?"

"I'm not wearing the sunblock."

"Whatever, Richard. You're a weirdo in my book."

"I'd like to see your book, Carla."

She runs, not in fear but evasion, runs like an athlete across the beach. Her footprints catch the full moon and fade as the wet sand absorbs her impacts. I let her go.

The bottle is empty when I get to the house. I drop it in the recycling bin by the door, letting it crash with the Evian and white wine bottles. I slip my shoes back on, ducking the hanging bits on the deck, and let myself in.

A giant brown blanket with a white tiger's head in the middle covers the wall across the front room. Ferns and leafy plants hang in pots. I smell a litter box and potpourri rising to a strange harmony above Indian massage music thumping backbeat. I walk through a small kitchen toward the back of the house, the sudden enclosure surreal from the outside. I have a purpose, I suppose. There's a reason I let myself in, a reason that has yet to come clear. How would I recognize the right decision? How could I live with it either way? Candlelight flips across the open door to the bedroom, light flickering for a meaning, trying to bring some mood or intimacy to this dark part of the house. An aquarium gurgles in the room, an odd sanitary sound like a hospital.

"Time to go, Marco," I say, stepping in.

The room is dim. Green light from the fish tank flecks the dark sheets of a low bed. Marco is on his back with his shirt off, his arms and legs stretched out like a sky diver. His head is in Mickey's lap, and she strokes his cheek, her hair hanging over him like a willow. Carla stands in the corner. She lights a candle with another candle and fans the scent of it toward her face.

"Let's go, Marco," I say.

Carla joins them on the bed and they lie together, silent, their faces dark in the low light.

"Marco, we need to leave!"

He stares at the ceiling between the two women, their hands touching his head and chest, their movements slow and caressing.

"It's now or never, Marco."

Mickey looks at me like I'm a painting on the wall, not alarmed or concerned, just studying.

"He's not leaving," she says, her voice deeper than I imagined.

"I'm not leaving, Rich," he says. "I'm not ever leaving." He chuckles. The women don't laugh.

I pitch the Coppertone bottle onto the foot of the bed, finding the release of it a relief to my hand. Carla and Mickey stroke his hair without noticing. They hum together, low, trancelike, their sound barely matching the bubbling of the tank.

The El Camino starts right up and reverse digs into the sand. I drop it into low and climb the steep driveway alone, the Monterey pines fanning at the coast, soaking up the wind in their regal lean toward the Pacific. She needs to know, I think. She needs to hear me say it, hear me aloud: "It's *you,* Sherrie. You are what's missing for me."

I crest the top with no fear of incidental collision, no fear of what's at stake, and accelerate north on the highway, north back to her.

We'll Talk Later

"Women want an intelligent mechanic and men want a distinguished nymphomaniac. That's what it comes down to!"

Merton slapped his hand on the steering wheel, finding new emphasis in the power of his Corvette compared to the bar at the Devon Links clubhouse that he'd been slapping his hand on minutes before. Rachel allowed him the moment, flipping the passenger visor down, then opening the mirror flap. She was used to his happy-hour assessments and felt the least she could do was give him a pause to repeat the statement in his head before she assailed him. She inspected her face, slanting her eyes and pitching her head to one side.

"I stumped you, didn't I? Didn't I!" Merton said, slapping the wheel again and showing his crooked teeth in a two-martini smile that appeared only when Rachel didn't want to see it. She sucked her cheeks in and blew a quick patronizing kiss at him.

They had moved to central Virginia from California three months before and everything was still part of the change: a grand unfamiliarity in the heavy dampness and lush pastures, the close-knit heat that baked through the humidity. The novelty of it all contrasted with the clear-skied brightness they'd been accustomed to in California, and they welcomed the change.

Neither of them were golfers. They had tried the game one time before they were married years ago but found it so hateful that they quit after three holes and drank in the clubhouse for a time equal to playing the remaining fifteen. Rachel thought golf was an abysmal sport, but she was drawn to clubhouses and so was Merton. They found them wherever they went and took them over, befriending the barkeep. They loved the quasi-rural separation of the manicured fairways beyond the wide clubhouse windows that put them outside Merton's documentary-film work and Rachel's event-planning business.

The Devon Links was established as their new clubhouse in Virginia. Its prime location outside town, midway between their offices and home, became a hub that all their explorations of the county spoked from in a slowly expanding radius.

★　　★　　★

A late-afternoon rain had come while they were in the clubhouse for happy hour, "tightening up," as Merton called it, before driving to a dinner party at the Russells'. The heat of the road vaporized the precipitation on impact, steaming into the dogwoods and tulip poplars that edged the two-lane highway. Dozens of box turtles, driven out of the ditches by the short downpour, crawled with surprising speed to a relative safety between the lanes, lining the center yellow stripe. Merton and Rachel had both seen the strange activity of the turtles before, and the wonder of it still intrigued them.

"So you think that you're an intelligent mechanic," Rachel said, wiping her eyelids with the tips of her fingers.

"I'm a technician. I'd say I'm a technician."

"And you feel I'm a distinguished nymphomaniac?" she asked, slapping the mirror flap shut.

"No, *we're* above it. We're in another group."

"We're in a group now?"

"It's a good group."

"So you think that I don't need an intelligent mechanic?"

"It's not *need*, it's *want*."

"I'm assuming you mean a craftsman of some sort when you say mechanic," she said.

Merton nodded, and she continued her questioning. "A man with a skill or talent – "

"Basic skill," he interrupted, "not super talent or art.

I mean basic male foundation, take-care-of-business-type skill: splitting wood, changing spark plugs, not some genius."

"But intelligent," she added.

"Yes, intelligent. Entertaining. Enough to hold a woman's attention."

"And you think this ultimate man is what every woman desires."

"I'm not accusing you or your gender, Rachel. What I'm saying is it's all a lot more basic. I think the issue is more basic . . ."

"What issue?" she yelled, feeling her gin.

"Want! The issue of want!" he yelled back.

They went quiet for a moment, having reached a volume unnecessary for the small interior of the car.

The steam cleared from the road exposing a straightaway, and Merton opened up the Corvette, sucking Rachel back in the deep seat with the brawn that made him a true believer in American muscle. They bolted through the late heat, the cicada racket audible in the maple trees, peaking in its crazy cycle.

"Watch the turtles!" Rachel said, but Merton didn't slow.

"When I say want, I don't mean a conscious yen or desire, I mean a basic physiological want – what the species wants from each other. We come up with all these explanations, these excuses for the encumbrance of being human, when really a woman wants a man that will take care of her and entertain her and provide for her with the intelligence to make her feel appreciated. And a man wants an upstart, good-looking home-builder with a discriminating but insatiable appetite for fucking."

"I'm going to vomit."

"Come on, babe . . ."

"No, really. Pull over, I'm going to vomit."

He braked hard and pulled to the side. Rachel had the door open before he stopped completely and she clambered out of the low seat, leaving the door swung wide as she stepped to the road edge and spewed clear fluid in the drainage ditch.

Merton stayed in the idling car watching her. He didn't go to her to touch her back or waist – the attention bothered her. It was better to let her do it on her own. He watched her skinny ankles and calves sprawl out as she held her dark hair back with one hand and straight-armed the small purse she had unconsciously brought along from the car with the other. The innocence of her inelegant posture comforted him, the life in her legs and ass. She hunched and heaved again, her legs twisting out with a feminine awkwardness that seemed natural and youthful to him until she turned around and her face showed the trouble of more years than her body.

"You all right, babe?"

"I'm fine," Rachel said, straightening her black skirt as

she dropped back into the cockpit seat. "Just gin on an empty stomach. I'll be fine."

"You still want to go to this thing?" he asked, feeling he wouldn't mind skipping the dinner party.

"I'm fine."

She yanked a tissue from the dispenser and wiped her face as Merton eased out on the highway, accelerating to a mild touring speed.

They had a few associates in town, but the dinner at the Russells' was to be their first social outing with locals.

Silas Russell was a timothy-hay farmer and tractor-equipment manufacturer. He had made millions from some harvesting implement he'd invented, a trowel-tooth attachment or something, Merton couldn't quite remember. Silas had told him about it in great detail at the clubhouse when they met, but he'd never really been able to envision the thing. Silas's scorecard-pencil rendering on a cocktail napkin looked like a prehistoric talon with bolt holes drilled through it. He couldn't see how the device was useful or how it made Silas so wealthy.

Merton agreed to dinner believing the invitation was small talk, but Silas confirmed the date a week later, handing him directions on a napkin, and Merton felt obligated.

"We'll let the wives visit and I'll show you the place," Silas had said, smiling his flat coarse face that widened and flattened more once he had Merton cornered. Rose was his wife's name; Merton hadn't met her yet. Rachel hadn't met either of them.

Silas's lifestyle interested Merton. He was fascinated by what people did with their money, and he saw the evening as possible material for an upcoming piece. *Lifestyles of the Rich but Not Necessarily Famous – The Unseen Glamour* was a working title he'd thought of. It needed to be trimmed down. Maybe *Hidden Wealth,* he thought.

Merton was on hiatus from his last film, a documentary on Nordic warfare, focusing on hand-to-hand combat. He didn't have the budget to travel to Scandinavia as he'd hoped, so he'd resorted to interviews with various professors at UVA and other local universities to explore the often unromantic aspects of ancient swordplay. He was now waiting for a response from a distributor considering the piece.

"What do you think of *Hidden Wealth*?" he asked, looking across the seat at Rachel.

"What?"

"As a title, *Hidden Wealth,*" he said.

Rachel shrugged and looked out the side window.

The sun was low and dull red, cutting ominously through the grayness above the beech and hickory trees. The rain had stopped up in the clouds again, and it would be hot through the night.

The sunsets worried Rachel, even in her dreamlike observance of the new environment. The starkness of the Virginia sun dropping nearly unnoticed, without the gold light or cloud display that she was used to, made her uneasy. The colors of the land were remarkable – the trees turning, but the clouds seemed to be part of the sky, a solid mass lacking definition or charm, all blue mopped up by the ubiquitous puce canopy that coated the state. She had yet to see spring; she'd heard the sky was clear then, but now it reminded her of the reason they moved from California.

Ash had been in the air – ash floating like snow particles and alighting delicately, piling up on the roads and roofs and cars, covering the neighborhood with an off-white blanket. She had walked through the light flakes that swirled and left her footprints obscured by the tiny wind of their sweep.

Chances are nothing will be as you imagine, she had thought, she had heard her own voice saying within her. But she had been wrong. That time her voice was wrong – her house had been taken. The house she had raised her son in. The house she had fought to keep after her divorce. The house she had remarried in and started again with Merton. It was gone, and only foundation stood in the ash. She had wept and held her face and looked at the sky, feeling that she would never be the type that looked to the sky, that prayer or desperation was weak. But she looked, and the sky was pewter-dark, the horrible eclipsed light of the sun pulsing heavy as blood through the ashes. Her home was lost, and there was no answer for it.

Rachel opened the mirror flap again and sighed, rubbing her eyes. She squinted a grimace at herself.

"People's needs change," she said, opening her purse to search for her makeup kit. "You may roll over everyone when you're working, laying out laws when they all adore you, when you're *directing*. But there's no law, no pre-ordained *want*, as you put it, that affects all people."

She coolly uncapped her lipstick pencil and went to work.

"This hackneyed philosophy that we are all victims to a basic want is shit."

She paused with the pencil and glanced quickly at him before she went on. "I could see if you were twenty maybe and living in Wisconsin you might think that but – "

"You think I'm being sexist?" Merton cut in.

"Well, maybe. I think you aren't allowing for growth. I think you aren't seeing that people keep growing and changing."

"Not everyone keeps growing," he said.

"Well, we'll apply your law to those unfortunates, but the other ninety percent of the population changes. You can't tell me that what a thirty-year-old woman wants and an eighty-year-old woman wants is the same thing, Merton – that's infantile!"

She punctuated her statements: slapping the mirror flap shut, recapping her lipstick, shoving it back in her bag.

"One minute you're puking in the ditch and now you're

attacking me," Merton said, wishing he could continue thinking about his next project.

"My point exactly." She laughed.

"What's your point exactly?"

"That things change!" she said.

They were silent. Merton turned on the map light and looked busily at the directions Silas had written with the same stubby pencil as he'd drawn his talon-trowel.

"That was Dexter Bridge," he said, thumbing behind them. "It should be coming up on the right, four four two."

Rachel scoffed at his sudden focus on the directions, but she made an effort to look for the number – the sooner they arrived, the sooner she could have another cocktail. She was due now.

Merton imagined the Russells' driveway differently. He pictured hedgerows, electronic gates, a call box maybe. But after the long turn from Dexter Bridge, cresting the hill as Silas had described, the entry to the Russell estate met the highway with simple dirt. Merton would've passed it, but Rachel saw the numbers and they turned in.

Acres of dark timothy fields spread gray-green on either side of the driveway, uniformly leaning toward a line of black brush and locust trees to the right that gathered the darkness in a band along the horizon. To the left, the hay stems and heads faded into mild hills that clung to the last light fighting through cloud cover.

Evening changed the land. The heat remained constant, but the moisture in the plants and grass blackened in lush shadows, holding a weight heavier than the sky. Mosquitoes came alive in the undergrowth of mulch and creek beds, lightning bugs blinked their courtship, cicadas maintained their machine of sound.

Rachel buzzed the electric window down a crack and took in the cut of smells and insect babel that rushed to the opening. She thought of her son. She saw his child body as he was in their old home, their California home. Bradley, untouched and vast as his father never saw him. His rockets, the model rockets. His fascination with propulsion and flight. Decals, spray paint. The way he corrected her when she called them sectional. "They're *multistaged,* Mom!" he would say, shaking his head as though he were twice his age before carrying his latest pride back to the hobby table. She loved his models, his passion, his interest when the world was still in front of him.

The dirt drive switched to pavement, clunking heavily on the sports car's tight suspension before going smooth. The jolt brought Rachel out of her recollection, and she realized her jaw had been clenched, her temples aching now from the pressure.

"What if Bradley could be here for Thanksgiving?" she said, seeing lights blink through a grove of black walnut trees ahead of them.

Merton clawed his hand through his hair and breathed deep.

"Please now, Rachel, let's not do this."

"I would love to see him," she said, lowering her voice and speaking to the gap in the window.

"We'll talk about it later," he said.

The plantation home came into view, looming proud. Four Doric pillars announced the doorway with tall, dark-shuttered windows filling the white wood walls on either side. Two enormous brick chimneys rose symmetrically from the pitched slate-tile roof, jutting like horns above the dormers.

"What is this, Monticello?" Rachel asked, admiring the massive house.

"Quite a spread." Merton laughed, happy to be addressing something physically before them.

Silas was in the driveway, walking from the trees toward the house. Merton recognized the man's unbalanced body, stilting along as if searching for a place to sit. A broken-open shotgun was slung over his right forearm.

"That man's holding a gun, Merton."

"That's Silas," Merton said, stopping the car near the brick walkway to the front steps and killing the motor.

Silas moved toward them, his wide head and thick upper body teetering on thin legs. He smiled, reaching Merton's window, and set his hand on the low roof.

"That's quite an outfit you got there!" he said, struggling

to lean down to their level. Rachel couldn't imagine how he might see her black skirt and top from his angle, but she said thank you. Merton glanced at her strangely.

"I bet she grabs her ass and runs off with ya," Silas said, chuckling.

"Yeah, she gets up and goes," Merton laughed out, patting the steering wheel.

"What are you saying?" Rachel asked.

"The car, babe. He's talking about the car," Merton whispered, opening his door.

They stepped out of the Corvette.

"This is my wife, Rachel," Merton said, sweeping an introductory hand toward her. Silas slipped the shotgun out of his arm crook and reached a handshake.

"It's good to know you," he said.

"Why the gun, Silas?" Merton asked.

"Oh, we got a bad mob of dogs runnin' around here." He motioned behind him to the hay fields beyond the trees that surrounded the house. "They breed with the locals, take out chickens, livestock, other dogs – just a bad pack that's runnin' loose."

"Really? I didn't think that stuff happened," Merton said as they walked toward the house.

"What stuff?"

"Wild dogs!" Merton laughed.

"Well, sure, we got this bunch now that's gotta be cleared out. We had a pack a few years ago that killed a calf on the Dexter property – took ten men to knock 'em out."

"Wow."

Merton was more impressed by the event of men killing dogs than the actual number it took.

Silas gently supported the open breech of the gun with his left hand as they walked, cradling the firearm as if it were the linked hand of a prom date. Rachel tried to ignore it. She wasn't fond of guns, and Silas's tender embrace of the dumb steel made her hum to herself, looking away to the unnaturally groomed hedge that lined the walkway.

"It's been hotter than billy crotch," Silas said, wiping his feet. "Rose likes to crank up the A/C."

Merton nodded, not knowing the expression but getting the point, as Silas opened the tall door and motioned for the guests to enter ahead of him into the vestibule.

The air-conditioning washed cold from the heart of the house, as if it had been on maximum the entire summer.

"Can I get you folks a cocktail?" Silas asked, shutting the door quickly behind them, hermetically sealing the house again from the muggy exterior.

"Martini, one olive," Rachel answered immediately.

"I'll have the same, please, thank you," Merton added, trying to soften Rachel's response with formality.

"Sounds good. I'll have Frederika shake up a few. Make yourself at home there in the den. I'm just gonna put this up." He patted the shotgun affectionately, then left the guests alone in the hall.

Merton went into the den as instructed, but Rachel lingered. She took in the long country-French bench and antique grandfather clock, the staircase that rose to her left, slanting up the wall to the second level, twenty feet above her head. Several oil paintings were hung randomly, somber Southern landscapes, cutting dark rectangular breaks in the cream-colored walls. The motif depressed her, the wainscoting, the bland colors, the stark cherry-wood dining table at the end of the house that she knew she would have to sit at. She could see Silas in the doorway to the kitchen. Over his shoulder, a board-thin black woman nodded to what he was saying, her hair oiled and stretched tight to her skull. Rachel inferred she was Frederika taking the martini order.

"I suppose it's a Southern thing," she said to herself, strolling the wood floor and looking closer at the paintings. The chill of the house unnerved her, the temperature so opposed to the outside. She felt horribly sober. She was stuck in a tank, she felt, looking out through the grim art on the walls. She wanted her drink; the gin would lighten things.

"Babe?" Merton's voice came from the den.

She walked back to him.

"What're you doing?" he asked, holding a photography book he had picked up from the coffee table.

"Just looking."

The den was pale blue. Theatrical drapes flowed without real function to the wood floor, a Colonial stiffness in their ironed creases. The fireplace didn't appear to have been lit in months, but wood was stacked neatly in a hamper beside it.

"Look at these prints," Merton said, pointing at the pictures on the wall. "They're those old Herring's fox-hunting scenes."

Rachel wasn't sure why she should recognize them, but she did.

"Huh," she said, looking at the bloodthirsty red-coated men encouraging hounds toward a scent.

"They're great, aren't they?" Merton said, admiring one of a gray horse and rider jumping a stone wall.

"Yeah. Great."

The art, the furnishings, the servant – they were all aspects of Virginia that she didn't want to be connected to. The land and charm of an older part of the country – the rich change in climate and history – suddenly crashed down on her, crashed down on the reason she left California. She had needed to be somewhere diametrically different. She had escaped something that was now unclear. She missed the spare Western land, the lean uncluttered views. She missed her son, and her temples ached again. She wanted to see him now.

Frederika came into the den with their martinis on a tray.

"Oh, thank you. That was fast," Merton said, setting the book down and taking his drink.

Rachel stepped from the picture on the wall and put her hand out. "My name is Rachel."

"Frederika." The woman smiled roughly, offering the drink tray instead of a handshake. Rachel brought the glass to her mouth and sipped a sizable amount. "That's a good martini," she said.

Frederika smiled and left the room.

"It might not be like you think," Merton said once they were alone.

"How do I think it is?" she asked coldly.

"I don't know. You just have that look."

"What look?"

"Forget it."

"How can you throw something like that out there?" she asked, sipping her drink again.

Footsteps came from the stairway, descending in a slow measured pace. The guests turned and waited, looking through the portal that framed a portion of the hall. The steps went on for what Rachel thought were minutes. She envisioned the number of stairs to the second floor, trying to imagine what Silas's wife looked like from the sound of her descent. She felt an obligation to freeze – to not take a sip or change position, as if moving would convict her of an insincerity. The footfalls hit solid wood floor, and after a moment Rose was in the doorway.

She was a small woman, as Rachel had assumed from her sound. European features, possibly French but more cold-weather, something mountainous in her eyebrows and small lips. Rachel guessed her to be forty-eight, but she could've been in her thirties at a glance.

"Oh great, you have martinis and I don't," Rose said, swinging wide of any first impression Rachel had of her diffidence.

The guests introduced themselves.

Rose's regal boldness and slanted Old Dominion accent suddenly brightened the austere house and made the fixtures seem warmer.

"Well, I hope Silas didn't startle you with his gun-toting. He fails to understand not all our guests are comfortable around firearms," she said, stating what Rachel gathered was an accustomed apology.

"Not to worry." Merton chuckled.

Rose then gave them a tour of the downstairs.

She carried the house with her, reigning in it with a swift, unexpected confidence as each long-floored room declared itself in dreary Virginia décor. The library, overtly masculine with hickory chairs, reading lamps, and leather-bound mail-order volumes. The slave-quarter guest room with a short, square-canopied bed and lone slatted chair. Rachel wanted to move on, finding the dourness of the rooms unsettling.

"We had trouble finding the right piece for this room,"

Rose said, presenting a huge freestanding closet that covered one wall of the study.

A shrill whistle sounded in a far part of the house, then Silas's voice followed, calling to the outside.

Both guests looked toward the sound.

"That's just Silas calling the dog in," Rose said, giving Rachel's arm a pat. "He thinks he has to screech like that. The poor thing comes in every night. I don't know why he has to make such a commotion . . . anyway." She brushed off the interruption, "Let's get you both another drink – a bird can't fly on one wing!"

The elated yips of the dog echoed through the house, then the scuffle of its claws, scrambling for traction on the wood floor, neared in the hall.

"Oh, here she comes," Rose said wearily, bracing herself for the dog to discover them.

A stringy, black McNab exploded into the room, its entire body wagging with the force of its excitement. It leapt on Rachel with its ears flat, lapping at her and nuzzling.

"Down!" Rose yelled, and the dog obeyed, leaving dirt paw prints on Rachel's black skirt.

"Oh, I'm so sorry, dear."

"That's okay," Rachel said, brushing at the marks. "What's her name?"

"This is Ed."

"As in *Edna*?" Merton asked, making a tentative attempt at petting the energetic animal.

"No, just Ed," Rose answered. "Silas named her after another dog. I think they've all been Ed."

Silas came in, his shirt changed. "*Ed!* Go on!" he yelled, and the happy dog skulked off in the direction of his pointing arm. "Sorry about that. I gotta bring her in 'cause of those dogs."

"Oh, she's fine," Rachel said, wishing Ed might stay to distract her.

The group moved back to the den, following the hostess's lead on the guided tour. Frederika brought more martinis and left again as the four sat, facing each other from hard, high-backed chairs.

"So when's your next movie comin' out?" Silas asked, rubbing his back on the chair as if it was a coarse-barked tree. Merton explained optimistically the process of awaiting distributorship.

"What's it about?" Silas asked, clearly bored by the marketing talk.

"Well, it's an exposé of sorts," Merton said, looking self-consciously at his cocktail before diving into his *filmmaker* tone that Rachel sometimes found charming. Tonight was different.

"I've tried to depict a candid representation of Nordic swordsmanship," he said, gathering no response except a nod from Rose, who rocked slightly, dwarfed by the size of her chair.

"I'm tired of choreographed Hollywood sword fights,

spinning ninja stuff. We need to see *real* sweat and exhaustion, labor, agony, not all these high-tech fencing moves and martial arts. These were heavy-bodied broadsword swingers, you know? They were brutal and powerful . . . Anyway, I hope it comes across. We'll see."

"So you found people to fight like that?" Rose asked, still rocking.

"Pretty much. I didn't have the opportunity to go overseas, but I think it'll work with what I have."

"I see," Rose said.

The four were quiet for a moment, then Rachel spoke.

"Merton and I were discussing something on the drive over," she said, drawing a quick look from her husband. "He feels that women want an 'intelligent mechanic,' I think is how he put it, and men – "

"Babe! Let's not get on that now." He cut her off.

"I'm interested in Rose and Silas's perspective," Rachel pushed.

"We'll talk about that later, okay?"

"You certainly seemed confident on the drive over."

Rose stood up and clapped her hands. "Supper should be set, if you all want to move into the dining room."

The duty to move on her instructions was a relief to the men, and they left the den together. The women followed.

"She's a real pistol," Silas whispered as they walked. Merton smiled back, hoping Rachel hadn't overheard.

"So, Silas, have you shot any of those dogs?" he asked.

"I clipped one, caught him out behind the pump house."

"Really?"

After the salad course, Rachel had a third martini while the others moved on to wine. The drink felt necessary to her tolerance of the situation, and she consumed it quicker than the one before, slipping away from the strain in her chest and the ache in her temples.

She began seeing the couple across the long cherry-wood table as impostors, actors on a strange set. Every word from Silas was perfect for his part, perfectly pompous and undereducated. Rose's acknowledgments were painfully peripheral – she struck Rachel as equally well cast for her role. There was a separation Rachel felt from the event that she began to explore. The situation was sadly comical: the host trapped within his own redneck construct, his urbane wife strong and erudite but poisoned by isolation and routine. They were hopeless, she felt; they lacked exposure, maybe, happening upon their lavish life by dumb luck.

"I got one of them Evinrude Bass-Tracker boats with a trolling motor," Silas said while they waited for the main course. "There's a sonar scanner or radar, something like that. It shows you where the fish are – the damn thing 'bout pulls 'em in for you, it's the darnedest. You just sit back, and the *boat* kills the fish."

"I'll be darned," Merton said, trying out the expression.

"I'll be darned?" Rachel repeated incredulously.

"You need to come out in the daylight, see the property," Silas went on, not noticing Rachel's comment. "I got a couple of them four-wheeler Jap jobs with the gun racks. I can take you down by the creek, we'll shoot some groundhogs."

"We'll have to do that." Merton chuckled.

"Are you kidding?" Rachel snapped. "What are you talking about? Killing fish, killing groundhogs, dogs!"

"Easy, honey," Merton said, glancing at the hosts. "She gets upset about animals." He laughed.

"So," Rose injected, "how did you find yourselves in Virginia?"

Rachel stared at her, unsure how to respond.

"Was it the climate?" Rose joshed.

"It's a long story," Merton said, hoping to move on.

"I feel alarmingly loaded," Rachel said, standing suddenly. "I need some air." She shoved her chair in and walked to the nearest exit. The side porch door gasped like a vacuum as she opened it, then she pushed through the second screen door and let it whack shut behind her.

"I hope I didn't upset your wife, Merton," Silas said.

"No, it's not you."

Rose stood and walked to the porch door.

"She'll be okay," Merton said. "Just let her be on her own. I don't want to trouble you with it."

Rose stood at the door, looking out as if she had forgotten

the porch was part of her house, as if Rachel had discovered it and deserved to be left alone in it.

Rachel sat on the hickory bench rubbing her temples. Moths manically dive-bombed the exterior light, trapped inside the screened-in porch. Cicadas and beetles careened around her, chopping their wings for spurting flights, smacking into the mesh walls and crawling stupidly across the screen.

Frederika came into the dining room with four platters of smallmouth bass, collard greens, and potatoes. She set two plates before the men, then filled the empty women's places with the others before disappearing into the kitchen again. The two men set in to eat.

"That screening doesn't seem to be keeping the bugs out, Silas," Rose said quietly, watching the show from her safe vantage point inside.

"Aren't you gonna eat, hon?"

"In a minute. You go ahead," she said, still watching the insects swarm Rachel in the harsh porch light.

"You should let Ed out there," Silas said to Rose. "She'll take care of those bugs. You should see that dog," he continued. "She wolfs those things down like giblets – boom boom, they're gone! You should see it."

"I'll be darned," Merton said.

The bare white bulb reflected off the white ceiling walls of the enclosed porch, encasing Rachel in a bright capsule of willing insects. Their display was beautiful, she thought, removed from the wet darkness beyond the screen and the frigid interior. She couldn't see anything but blackness beyond the mesh and the silhouettes of insects that couldn't find their way in. She focused on them, their numerous colors and chubby bodies, antennae fanning out like ferns. Bats shrilled in the dark. Dogs barked far off that might have been the wild dogs, she didn't know. She was content to not move, to not dare going out into the night or return to the inside. She would stay in between, apart, knowing within her blood that she would never see her son. Just as her old home was gone, all of it was gone – all of that life behind her had been taken, and the sky that followed her here had no answer.

Thirty Head of Killers

Souli's in worse shape than me. He got on that sotol shit
last night and went right out to lunch. I had a taste of it
and kept to beer – you never know with those liquors that
aren't legal in Texas.

"¡El abuso de consumo es muy malo para la salud!" he was
saying all night, reading it off the label. But he isn't saying it
anymore. He isn't saying anything. He's just leaning against
the tack shed, staying in the shade like a dead man in
sunglasses and his Guatemalan palm hat. The thing weighs
nearly ten pounds. He creases it like a regular straw, but it's
made out of those palm leafs. He fell in the creek with it
in Alpine, and the sun cooked it till his head sweat got a
fungus growing inside the crown. The thing's been rotting
on his head for weeks. He lets it air out at night, and you
can smell it in the dark just growing. But he still wears it.

Best hat he's ever owned, he says. He's standing there in it, leaning on the tack shed looking like he might give out at any point and just disintegrate to a pile of shit in the dirt.

His truck was impounded last night, and we're late because of it, so Reed is putting us on the killers. Reed doesn't want to know why the truck was impounded or why we're still in our Friday night duds. He knows we smell like Mexico, and the rest doesn't matter, we're late. So when it comes down to who's gonna be culling the killers this morning, he assigns the unfortunate bastards that aren't on time, me and Souli.

It's hot already. The humidity will get a guy in full sweat before the sun's up – I go through four shirts a day. The trailers are here at the holding pens, but they haven't unloaded the horses yet. The drivers are sleeping in the cabs of the two trucks. I guess they drove right through the night, hauling the four-hundred-odd miles from El Paso to Del Rio while we were across the river in Acuña, laughing at the four-nippled chick that was sweet on Souli.

We were on our way even before Burger passed us the word that there was work to be done today. Burger said it came straight from Reed that the whole crew had to be at the holding pens by eight A.M. That'd give everybody a chance to sleep in, he said.

We haven't had a night out in weeks, bustin' our asses with wagon work up in Alpine, and after the big company move to Del Rio yesterday, we were due to drop the reins a bit. Burger told us we had to work, but there wasn't any quit in us at that point; me and Souli were already half-tuned on Bohemias and aimed at Boystown, Acuña.

Souli was yellin' *"¡Yo voy toda la noche!"* to all the whores. I could hear him yellin' down the hall. Gray doors and nap wall-to-wall that make sparks fly off your hand on the doorknobs. I ducked in with a girl that might be eighteen, playing up the high school thing with eighties airbrush posters of harlequins crying and lace shit all over her room. Little dolls and white crap, frilly curtains over windows that were just phony frames nailed to the Sheetrock walls. It all smelled like mangoes or some fruit. I forget what she called herself, Bettina or something. Something almost American. I had a little trouble with how young she was, but I got it all done. Souli was screamin' out front, drunk by the pool table, yelling that he'd been waitin' on me for twenty minutes. He was calling the four-nippled chick *"la vaca."* That's when we had to leave. Border-town locals don't go for gringos calling their whores cows. I can't blame them. We got out like raped apes, jumping in some cab, and hit the Texas side of the river by two A.M. Souli puked in the parking lot, then said he was good to drive back to Bracketville. It's hard to stop Souli when he's set on driving. I thought of four-waying the fucker with the grass rope in the truck and chunkin' him in the bed, but he already had it running. The Del Rio cops pulled us over for a taillight, but more likely our New Mexico plates were what boned us. Not even the smell of Souli's hat could cover up what we'd been doing, reeking like Hell's brewery. They arrested us and threw us in the tank overnight with a bunch of screaming Mexicans that were beatin' on the walls and the little square window in the door. The cops took everybody's shoes and belts – so we wouldn't kill ourselves, I guess.

The truck was impounded. There was hungover paperwork this morning and slick bondsmen waiting, slipping around for their ten percent. It's a wonder we made it to the pens only half an hour late.

Reed and Burger walk over to the tack shed. Reed's fiddling a fiador knot with his big hands and not looking at us.

"We need a double for Blueboy and anything else that's rideable," he says, the brim of his hat hiding his eyes. "And we've gotta get some background horses for that big town scene they added, anything that's halfway sound and not too humpy will do." That's all he says. Burger smiles like a little pig behind him, and they walk away.

Me and Souli grab our woods out of the tack shed and trudge our sorry asses over to the arena.

Low-budget non-union jobs like this get the boss edgy – puts the guy in a bind, giving him X amount of dollars that add up quick in wages and rentals. But then the director or producer or somebody demands more horses. Horses that haven't been seen already. You can only make twenty head look like fifty for so long, then it gets tricky, risking continuity errors that'll make you look like an idiot. You go through Polaroids and shit, trying to remember which horses were featured. Stuff that could've been shot a month ago, but then a year later when you watch the movie on your motel TV, it's right back-to-back – the hero riding into town on a bay horse and then riding out on a sorrel. That kind of mistake makes a boss jumpy.

Anyway, we need more horses. We can't afford California stock or good local rentals, so Reed intercepted these loads that are headed to slaughter from El Paso: killers. He figures we might get lucky and pick up a few for fifty or sixty cents a pound.

Burger and the other guys have already set up a two-hundred-gallon stock tank in the arena. The drivers unlock the trailer gates, then go back to sleep in their trucks. The rest is left to me and Souli.

We wire pipe-corral panels from the back of the trucks to the arena gate, making a chute to funnel them in. Then we drop the ramps.

The killers shuffle around, peering out from inside, their ears all pricked up. They sniff the ramp, then one or two start easing out, then a couple more. Movement travels through them, and suddenly the pace picks up, building to a flow until they're blowing out like yellow jackets from a hole in the ground, rocking the trucks, then hitting the dirt and boiling dust. They churn up a cloud in the arena that hides them all for a minute, their heads and legs breaking out here and there, a couple of them wailing and carrying on, snortin' at the strange place and feeling maybe free for a spell from being stuck in the trailers all night.

The dust clears out and they surround the tank, fighting for the water like feed, timid or bold, all in a sweat lathered from being against each other. They dive their heads in and suck. The tank isn't big enough for all of them at once.

"That's about the thirstiest mob I've seen," Souli says, and I agree. We sit up on the rail to take a head count, and both come up with thirty, watchin' them swarm the tank, mashing together in a wild huddle. One blaze-faced sorrel turns wicked and drives his hip into another, then squeals and kicks, connecting with a pock! Their heads swing up from the sound, and big streams of water pour from their mouths. They scramble and readjust, then sink their heads back into the tank to drink.

They drain it dry in under ten minutes. Two hundred gallons. Then they settle a bit.

"There ain't a number one in the bunch except that big bay with the snip," Souli says as we look them over. He's right, one big bay gelding with a bright snip on his nose stands out from the remuda. I'm amazed Souli has enough salt left in him to pay attention, but he's got an eye, no matter how bad a shape he's in. He's probably *forgotten* more about horses than most will ever learn. But I can tell he's dreading having to get on any of them. That sotol is backing up in him; he's sweatin' just sitting on the rail.

There's nothing grass-fat or muscled in the group. Nothing headed to France, that's for sure. They're all grade two or three: common west Texas stock horses and Mexican ranch-work types, nothing that will bring more than forty cents a pound. Low-yield dog food and tallow. Worm-bellied, ribby, dull-coated sorry-looking swaybacked things. None of them can be under sixteen years old except the big bay with the snip.

We cull eight right off the bat that don't have a chance: one's front feet are separated at the coronary band, his hooves just about sloughed off – I can't believe he even made it off the truck. A couple navicular cases gimp around on tiptoe; three are foundered so bad, trying to walk on their hind legs, that they just lie down to take the weight off. And the last is just so old and poor he can't be used, not on a movie set anyway.

We push them all into the two holding pens that branch off the arena, possibles in one, culled in the other.

Souli throws a hoolihan loop over the one blaze-faced bully that's kickin' the shit out of everybody, and we shut him off by himself. Of course he screams and cries on his own. He doesn't mind beatin' the hell out of everyone, but he wails for them once he's alone.

We're trying to beat the heat here, get through all of them by twelve or one before the temperature is god-awful. We both hurt from our night out, but we bear down and go to work.

There are two grays in the twenty-two head that are left, the only possible doubles for Blueboy like Reed wants, but they're too small to match him and, looking closer, we find melanoma knots under their tails. Grays always get that cancer, so we pass on them. We cull the blaze-faced kicker too. He'd just be trouble.

Every one of them has high ringbone welts on their pasterns and old, hard splints on their legs from the pounding they've had in their lives, not all unsound, just riddled with wear-and-tear scars from punchin' cows out of cedar brush and years on rocks. Some even have white scar hair on their withers and girths from time under saddle, poor-fitting ones, but at least we know they've been ridden at some point. Ridden hard.

None of them are too keen on us handling them, and they storm around the holding pen like range cattle until the two of us close in; then their manners come back, and they remember how to be with men. You can see the switch in their eyes when they realize there isn't any other way. Everything comes back from what they know of giving in, and the difference between a herd that runs together and a herd that's thrown together comes clear; the safety in numbers instinct only works when they're not afraid of *each other*. They know work and men and most of them welcome our touch once the blood calms in them; they only have so much to belong to, and they let us halter them without much trouble. But how a horse is on the ground and how he is when you're on his back are two different things.

A couple of the guys are working on a wagon next to the barn, lubing hubs or something, and Reed and Burger are tinkering on some harness at the tack shed. I'm sure they're watching us out of the corner of their eye as we step onto the first two. Burger always stirs things up to get on Reed's side of things, and I know he'd love to see us get dumped in the arena by some common piece of shit horse.

A lameness we hadn't seen on Souli's first mount shows up after three steps, and mine roars like a vacuum cleaner when we hit a trot, lung disease or something. We both move on to others.

It would be a miracle for any of them to walk off and be a solid-broke horse. We can't hardly blame them for being squirrelly, but they have to be solid to be usable – that's the bottom line. Even if we come up with something that might turn out being good and quiet with work, there isn't enough time to put in on them. I think the whole deal's probably just Reed's punishment for us being late, instead of a real job. But we have to go through with it.

"We aren't gonna find a thing in this mob," I say to Souli, and he just nods, looking more like a corpse than before.

The drivers sleep through the whole thing. We take the geldings out one at a time into the arena and find their flaws, working them in circles, pushing them through their gaits until they reveal why they're on the truck — unsoundness, madness, age.

Souli gets a stocking-legged chestnut that humps up and hops like a kangaroo. He walks two steps, leaps like an idiot, then freezes, then he leaps again. Souli just gets off him and walks him back to the culled pen.

We both know it's all a joke. There isn't one in the herd that will be worth a damn, so it's every man for himself. I try to find the more docile outcasts with gentle eyes, hoping Souli takes the dominant waspy ones. There just isn't much point risking everything on thirty head of killers. I know Souli's picking his mounts carefully; I can see him scanning over them. It's funny the amount of effort put in on laziness and self-preservation, pitting our judgment of horseflesh against each other trying to find the quietest to ride. Partnership only goes so far in this gig. Souli stood by me with the Mexicans in the drunk tank last night, but when it comes to jumping on a scared strange animal, you're on your own, and it's better if the other guy gets nailed on a maniac.

The main horse I'm avoiding is the big bay with the snip that we both spotted early on. He's the only half-decent-looking animal in the group, but I don't trust his eye: a piggy eye, too small for his size. He cuts a wedge through the herd like a predator, unafraid and muscled. He shines from good feed, his feet are trimmed, he's sound. He doesn't belong with the others. There's a reason he's on the truck, a reason

I don't want to figure out. You don't just kill off a horse like that.

I catch a little dun gelding with a heart-shaped star on his forehead. He looks pretty harmless. I figure I'll busy myself on him for a while and see if Souli takes the big bay with the snip, but he doesn't. He had an opportunity to halter him, but he goes after a pigeon-toed roan instead. I know he doesn't want any part of Snip either.

My little dun turns out all right. He's old but doesn't have any mean bones in him. I tool him around the arena, hit a jog, a lope, stop, turn. He stands good and has a fair mouth. I ride him back as a keeper.

"Dunny here wants to be in pictures," I say to Souli.

He's found another dud in the roan, who takes the bit and tries to run off with him, grabbing his ass and motoring across the arena.

"Whoa, you son of a bitch!" he yells at him, cranking his head around to circle him until he stops. He steps off and kicks him in the belly, then leads him back to the killers.

"This dumb son of a bitch ain't too clear on the situation," Souli says, stripping the saddle and bridle off; then he kicks him in with the culled.

After a couple hours, we're down to four. Our only keeper is the one little dun, and he isn't anything too special.

The heat is startin' to bear down, and we're both kinda fed up. Souli notices one strip-faced Mexican horse has a

cut above his hock; we figure him to be the one that got
kicked at the water tank.

"I better clean that up a little," he says.

He halters the sorry thing and leads him out the gate
toward the water hose, leaving me with the last three to
choose from: a tricolored paint, a yellow gelding with a
peanut ass, and the big bay with the snip. I see how Souli
works it: He's a little too eager to doctor a doomed horse
– there isn't any point. He pounced on the opportunity
so that he wouldn't get stuck on the bay, I know it. No
matter which one I take out now, he'll take the other and
leave Snip last for me.

"Hey, I can doctor that horse," I yell to him over the rail.
He turns and rips me a wicked smile and keeps walking –
the son of a bitch, he's worked it all out.

I could cull the yellow horse right off and ride the paint
and leave the big bay for Souli; that's an option that's a little
unfair to the yellow horse. But then I think, Fuck it, if that
chickenshit Souli isn't gonna get his powder wet, I'll just
show him and ride the big bay horse right now! I don't
know what's come over me, the heat and all of it. My
heart's going, and I'm a little fried about the whole deal,
but I'm not gonna be duped.

I halter the big bay, throw my wood on him, and cinch
him up. I feel like hammered dog shit – the sweat's clean
through my shirt – but the chore is almost done. Even if
the son of a bitch turns me into the old human dart head-first

in the dirt, I don't really care, I just want to be through with the whole thing.

I look at Snip's eye again though and I worry. A small round eye, a hard wrinkle underneath. There's something kind of playful and innocent but sharp and crooked like a goat's. I slip the Tom Thumb bit in his mouth, pull the bridle over his ears, and buckle the throatlatch. I lead him out into the arena and step up on him.

He's a big horse, sixteen hands and balanced, but on his back he's a lot narrower than I thought. There isn't anything too secure about him. I sit deep in his back and rein him two-handed like a colt.

I walk him in a slow circle feeling him out, tipping his head to flex his neck. I stop him and stand for a second, then squeeze him up. He responds smoothly, and I ease him into a little jig, still sitting deep in his back, moving with him, circling. He's quiet and steady, striding out in a nice jog. I check him, and he stops straight. Maybe somebody put the wrong horse on the truck, he seems pretty honest, but I'm still not a hundred percent.

I see Souli leading the Mexican horse back to the arena, and Reed and Burger are walking with him. They all come up to the railing and look on as I smooch Snip into a walk again.

"I think somebody might've made a mistake with this horse," I say.

Reed looks at Burger, and they laugh.

"He seems all right so far," I say, easing him into his comfortable jog.

"Why don't you kick him into a lope," Reed says, and he laughs again.

It might be the hangover that's got me bold, that and the resentment for the chore. But on Reed's suggestion, I cluck to Snip and squeeze his sides with my heels.

There's always a moment when things come clear, where you stop thinking and just react. It's either fear or stupidity or cockiness that brings on a realization that you're a man with limitations. And that happens in the transition from trot to lope on Snip: He lunges with such power and violence that I'm nearly unseated from the force, and whatever time I've put in on horses takes over, sticking me to him without making any choices.

The horse swallows his own head; it disappears between his front legs and he breaks in half, groaning like a bull elk. I pull with everything, but his head and neck are locked down out of sight, and all I see is my arms, my hands, and the saddle as the animal erupts beneath me, focusing all his ability on shedding me like a deerfly, clinging and pulling. I taste the impacts of my life in the pounding, a flavor like my own cartilage in bouts with concrete and car wrecks. Concussion and fluids jam through my tailbone and neck, ripping my body apart, and I shove my chin down and clench my teeth. All sense of the arena is gone, the heat, the men watching me. I fight for my life, and the horse feels none of it. I am his. He owns me and works me like a speed bag, throwing everything into me from the hard bend in his back with a punch and a punch and another punch. He leaps and kicks, sun-fishing and striking, then barely touching the ground to spring and grunt, breaking a flex and crack that slaps me back against his hip and makes me question survival.

"Hang it in 'im, C.L.!" I hear from the railing, but the distance is like an ocean, like another life I'll never see. The ground looks safe, the ground blurring by and flashes of the railings and the sky. It's only me and the horse, everything else is erased. Everything else is gone, and his power whips my body across his back, numbing me with a weightless ferocious rhythm that cuts my senses from fear or thought.

And then it's over. Like that. It's done, and Snip stands still.

I'm still on his back. We're still in the arena. I can feel his barrel expanding between my knees, and everything is quiet. Sweat is in my eyes and on my hands. My whole body's wet, and I heave to catch air.

I have no idea why he stopped or how I'm still on him. We just stand there blowing.

The sound of Reed, Burger, and Souli comes to me, their voices hopping across the arena like a flock of grackles. They're laughing like nothing's ever been so funny, all of them just pissing themselves.

"I was markin' you out pretty good till you lost your hat!" Souli yells.

I didn't even notice I'd lost my hat. I step off dazed and lead the big horse over to it, each step tying me up. My knees are shaking, my hands hurt, my neck. Everything is knotted in a solid ache like I've been run through a mixer. I pick my hat out of the dirt and brush it off, then put it back on and walk to the railing.

"What do you think of Drifter?" Reed says, nodding toward Snip. He laughs again and Burger joins in.

"Drifter?" I ask.

"His name's Drifter," Reed says. "He's our buckin' horse from Sonora. A stuntman hauled him in last night after you boys went on your little tear. We thought we'd throw him on the truck with the others this morning just to see if you'd notice." He laughs again. "He's nice and quiet at a walk, but if you ask him to lope he'll pitch – he goes ten seconds and quits, but he's got some good action, I'll say that. You rode him out pretty good, C.L. You done pretty good."

They all three laugh together.

"Well, you can put him back on the truck!" I tell him, but then I laugh too. It feels better to laugh.

We quit for the day and help the drivers load the culled back on the trailers. They pull out and continue on to their final destination, kicking up dust and clattering down the farm road, leaving us with the little dun and Drifter.

"I knew that horse was loaded," Souli says once they're

gone. "You stayed in the middle of him pretty good, C.L."

"I don't know if I had much to do with it," I tell him. "All I know is I'm not gonna be late tomorrow!"

Souli laughs. "Drifter must've knocked you into the wrong end of the week," he says. "We're off tomorrow. It's Sunday!"

"Thank Christ," I say.

We walk back across the dirt lot to the tack shed and shade up from the afternoon sun.

Ravendale Loop

Brynne trails her husband through Value-Op, their un-wieldy carts dwarfed by the expansive shopping complex.

"It's not that I care . . ." Tiny starts up, leaning with an acquired hunch to hide his bulk. "It's not that it's sinful or wrong," he continues, "it's the overt display that screws me up. Did I just say that? That's what it is, Brynnie. I don't give a shit that they're fucking around – just don't do it in my face, you get me?"

"Maybe they won the drawing?" Brynne suggests.

"They didn't win the drawing."

"Somebody has to win it . . ."

"Brynne, they didn't win the drawing, okay! They're fooling around in a public place. They're celebrating their I-don't-know-what, their boldness. They're not winners of a prize! Come on! How could they both win it, anyway? How would that work?"

"All I'm saying is there might be an explanation for it that's – "

"The explanation is they're fucking around! Bottom line!"

"That is *innocent!* Would you let me speak, please? There might be a legitimate reason for them being together. That's all I'm saying."

They walk through the warehouse aisles, passing stacked cases of wholesale products, bargain bins, racks of palletized goods that tower on either side. They skim over the merchandise with the same pedestrian interest as the other locals that mill around them.

Brynne feels apart from the other shoppers, even though her cart is just as full and she recognizes neighbors on every visit. She feels an individuality that shines in her cheeks, in her bony wrists, her straight hips. She's in an in-between period, she feels, a parenthesized hiatus in the town of Ravendale. She grew up here.

"I'm just glad the kids weren't witnessing it," Tiny says, jutting his elbows and leaning on his cart.

"What kind of comment is that?"

"I'm just glad they're not victim to the indecency that's being paraded around!"

"You've really gone off the deep end with this, Tiny."

"I know what I saw, Brynnie. This isn't some goddamned dream I'm in here!"

"There's no need for that . . ."

"Don't talk to me like the kids!"

"I'm not, sweetie. I'm not – "

"Don't slip into that patronizing shit."

"*Tiny,* we've got to get Liss and Cubby from school!"

"I know we do!"

"Just let down a little, okay? Let down, honey. It's not that big a thing, even if it's true, even if you saw some adulterous 'display.' It's nothing to get so wound up over."

"You can't see it, you don't have any idea where I am, do you?" he says.

"Let's just drop it, okay?"

The bottleneck at the cashiers continues out to the cars in a whirlpool current of exodus and inflow as the vehicles battle in the acres of parking.

"Ooh! Careful, sweetie!" Brynne says as they back the Ford L T D out of its space. Tiny stands on the brake pedal, nearly hitting a passing car. She waves to the other driver, mouthing "sorry" through the window of the sedan; then they back out.

They pull free of the Value-Op melee and accelerate onto Ravendale Loop, rising up the on-ramp of the elevated thoroughfare. They roll the windows down.

"What's he thinking?" Tiny blurts, settling into the flat stretch between the shopping complex and Ravendale Junior High. "What does he think, that they'll *run off* together?"

Brynne turns to the side window as he continues.

"It's a joke – the guy thinks he's got everyone buf-faloed. The old 'friend of the husband.' He thinks people would never guess, that it would go unnoticed? It's embar-rassing."

Brynne looks at him, seeing his thick forearm hair on end in the wind. She squeaks down in the vinyl seat and wedges herself against the door as far away from him as possible. She watches his mouth move, trying to see any part of the man that won her. She turns back to the window.

The town houses transform to mills, then to crop rows, blinking by in unison with the guardrail posts of the elevated highway. She remembers how they used to drive the narrow farm roads below them that run thin between the flood ditches, dead-ending into right-angle turns, then continuing on again straight. There were never any curves, only ninety-degree turns and straight road. She always imagined she was a rook, traversing the giant grid in straight lines, sweeping the distance like a hand gliding the piece across a board. But now she's floating above it, cutting a diagonal path that she never would have imagined before the construction of the loop. She misses the farm roads.

"You could never please a woman like her, you know? You couldn't win. She'd lure you like a hot pie and burn the shit out of you. Did I just say that? That's what it is, like a peach pie on the counter – too hot to cut.

"A guy might get a taste, she'd let him in after all the

pleading, the notes, little secret phone calls . . . She'd give him a nip, and he'd just shrivel up like a schoolboy, get right in her shirt pocket. He tells her he loves her, that she's everything to him, and she's thinking of some movie star, checking her watch while he's pounding away – masturbating in her, trying to get his hooks in. And she'd let him, she'd let him try his heart out even if she couldn't get off on a *horse's* prick."

Brynne hears none of it. She floats past the bland hood of the sedan, inhaling the land's silence, all her heart in the fields.

Felicity and Cubby stand fifteen feet apart, waiting for their parents to pick them up. Their friends have already left on the bus.

"There they are!" Cubby says, seeing the LTD exit the elevated loop and circle down the off-ramp to ground level. He squints his eyes, enhancing the fantasy of an undercover reconnaissance mission, and springs to the azalea bushes that edge the school offices.

Felicity ignores him, reaching inside her overalls to scratch at her training bra.

The sedan bounces into the lot and stops at the curb.

"Where's your brother, Liss?" Brynne asks through the open window.

"In the bushes . . . What's all this stuff?"

"We just came from Value-Op."

"There's no room to sit!" Felicity says, opening the door.

Tiny stares straight through the windshield.

"Just get in, there's room!" he says.

"Cubby!" Brynne calls. "Come on, sweetie, we've got to go."

Tiny mashes the horn with his full palm.

"Come on, damn it. If I have to go out there and get him . . ."

"Here he is. Here he is."

Cubby appears from the bushes. He hangs his head and drags his leg like a wounded man to the car.

"What's all this stuff?" he asks, opening the door.

"Get in!" Tiny screams.

He throws his backpack in and uses his whole body to shut the door behind him.

"I don't want to hear it right now, Cubby!" Tiny roars from the front seat, merging back onto the loop. "This isn't about you, you get me? You are far away right now. I'm discussing something here without interruptions! You understand?"

Cubby nods from the back, watching the pavement outside the window.

"Hail, Caesar," Felicity says to herself, looking out the opposite side.

"Let down a little, honey," Brynne says to Tiny. "Don't get so wound up, sweetie, please."

"Wound up! We're discussing something here. Are we not discussing something?"

"The kids, Tiny . . ."

"Fuck the kids! This isn't about the kids."

"Please, Tiny . . ."

"No! No 'please, Tiny,' no 'let down, Tiny.' Who's the adult here, huh? Who's the goddamn adult in this car?"

Brynne doesn't answer.

"I'm talking to you, Brynne!"

"Don't make me get into this, it's nothing to do with me. It's bygone, for Pete's sake . . ."

The swing sweeps a flat arc from Tiny's shoulder and sinks full force into Brynne's face. Her back arches. Her hands go to her face. She collapses forward below the glove box.

"Oh, God," Tiny says.

The car is stopped in the small shoulder space midspan on the loop.

"Oh, Christ, Brynnie. Baby?" He reaches to her across the seat, touching the exposed part of her back where her blouse has untucked.

"What happened?" Felicity screams, pulling herself half-way into the front seat.

"Sit down!" Tiny's voice rips out. "Both of you just sit down now."

Brynne drifts. She doesn't feel the awkward position of her body. She's able to drift in the pain, holding everything close. Thickness in her face, blood in her teeth. She weeps. She holds in the heap she forms, twisting small until she's a fetal ball on the floor.

"Brynnie . . . Baby? . . . Fuck!" Tiny hits his hands on the wheel and slumps forward. His fingers spread open, white.

Cubby and Felicity freeze in the back. They watch a car pass and slowly diminish on the highway. The fading sunlight turns gold and comes sideways into the LTD.

"I thought I could hide . . ." Brynne mumbles from the floor, her words wet.

"What, baby?" Tiny says, his head on his hands.

"I thought I could hide out in the tule fog . . ."

"What are you talking about, Brynnie? Sit up, please. Can you sit up? I'm sorry. I'm sorry." He holds his head.

Brynne doesn't move, her voice faint.

"There was nothing to rush for . . . They were pulling ticks from my head. I was crying. I must've been crying . . . Splinters, wires in my pores. I said, 'You shun her because she arouses you, because she's your own' . . . I couldn't feel it even seeing it slip out. I couldn't feel it . . . I screamed and ran with it all dripping across the mattress . . . I ran, pulling with my hands . . . I was in the fields. They had already trimmed the heads, it was just straw. Wheat straw. The stems jabbed at my legs, my feet . . ."

"What are you saying? Oh, God. What's happened, what's happening?" Tiny yells, his face imploding.

Brynne slowly rises from the floor and kneels to face the back, her hands on the seat.

"They found me out there in the stubble," she says, her eyes barely open. She looks miles past the car. "I remember hearing them crunch through the stobs, I could hear it in the earth . . . I knew I wouldn't escape."

"Brynnie?" Tiny begs.

"No," she says. "No."

Wax

"Have you ever had a coning?"

"What?"

"Cone your ears."

"I don't know what you mean . . . Cone?"

She was stirring lentils on a hot plate, the smell blending with the patchouli oil she wore and the incense that permeated the houseboat.

"It's amazing," she said. "It draws all the cerumen from the auditory canal . . ."

"Do what?"

"The wax."

He sipped a cup of chai, something he'd never had, and tried to imagine how things could evolve between them. He had come this far, making it into her home. She was flirtatious but mannered, obscured by interests that were foreign to him. The aromas bothered him. The metaphysical bookshelf. The chakra chart on the wall. The closet bathroom with a curtain for a door.

"What's this cone?" he asked her, looking out at the water that still held some light from the sun going down.

"I have a few there by the window." She pointed with a wooden spoon across the cramped space.

He stood up from the couch and stooped under the low ceiling, the tide rocking. He put the cup down on the coffee table and walked the two steps to the window.

"You set it in the ear, and light the end," she said, sipping the lentils from the spoon. "Mmm, these are dreamy. You like lentils?"

"You light the end?"

"Yes."

"On fire?"

"Yes." She laughed, moving to the cabinet over the sink.

He picked up one of the cigar-sized cylinders and rolled it in his hand, feeling the hollow waxed parchment that tapered on one end. He smelled it.

"How does it work?"

"It's the heat. The heat draws it out. You should try it, you'll be amazed. People use those peroxide cleaners, you know, those little kits with the plunger? Those are horrible – blasting everything out with water! They can actually damage the inner ear. I've heard people ruptured their drums, can you imagine? This draws it out."

She pulled her hands away from each other as if stretching putty between them.

He was unsure.

"You forget how your hearing was. You think it's clear now, but there's years of buildup in there, you know? You have to try it. Afterward, the sounds, it's incredible – everything, little wisps."

Little wisps? he thought.

"Does it hurt?"

"No, you don't feel a thing. Here, we'll do it after we eat."

She had filled two handmade ceramic bowls and handed him one.

"This looks great." He hated lentils.

They sat on the couch holding the bowls, the table too low to eat from.

"How long have you lived here?" he asked, choking down the bland beans.

"All my life. I've only been on *this* boat for a few years, but I grew up on the pier. My mother had a boat on the north side; I was born there."

"Really. You were born on a houseboat?"

"Mm-hmm. Natural birth, all of that."

"Wow." He wondered what it would take to get in her pants. "So I guess you're pretty used to being on the water."

"It's just a part of me, the whole place. It's a big family

out here, you know? Everyone's so in touch with who they are, what they want. It's wonderful."

He nodded, pretending it meant something to him.

"Do you have any beer?" he asked.

"No." She chuckled. "We can get some from the store if you want."

He sensed a suspicion in her tone.

"No, that's okay. I just thought if you had some . . ."

"No." She went back to eating.

"I've never been on a houseboat," he said.

He wondered if it was all worth his while, chatting. If his intentions were obvious. He was already turned off by the way she talked, the way she smelled, her precious surroundings. But she was exquisite. She was what he called deluxe, a natural talent. His recent dry spell had him aching. He imagined her in something skimpy, seeing her in a motel room or a hot tub – some place designed for fucking. He imagined her breasts beneath her cotton dress, wondering if she might beg him to take her from behind, if she might squeal like a little girl.

"So, are you ready?" she asked, taking the empty bowls to the sink.

"What?"

"Obviously you are."

"What are you talking about?"

"The *coning!*"

"Oh, right."

"You'll have to lie on your side."

He stretched out on the couch hoping it might lead to something, keeping his stomach flat.

She tore two pieces of tinfoil in the kitchen area and picked up a box of matches.

"This catches the ashes," she said, taking one of the ear cones from the window ledge and punching it through the foil. She knelt down next to him and reached both her arms to his head, gently holding his ear with one hand and inserting the cone with the other.

He was aroused. He could see her brassiere through the gap of her sleeve, her hips snug in the kneeling position.

"You have to hold it there while I light it."

He didn't want her to take her hand away. He thought of grabbing her.

He supported the cone and she lit the end.

"Now keep it upright, and don't move around. It takes about fifteen minutes."

She stood up, dropping the matchbox on the table, and went back to start the dishes.

The flaming tube jutted from his ear, reflecting in the window. He saw the darkness outside, little orange candles and knickknacks crowding the sill. He was stuck, the entire event unnatural to him, every element. He wanted a cigarette, a cocktail. He wanted her to kneel by him again.

"Is it straight?" he asked, hoping she would come back.

She nodded, saying it looked good from where she was. He could hear the water running.

"You're on your way!" she said.

It struck him that she had no reason to be interested in him. He knew nothing about her. She might like women, for all he knew. He could be falling back into the tragedy of friendliness, the circle that never considered sex.

"See, you don't feel anything, do you?" she said, turning the water off.

"No. You're right."

A current rolled the boat, and he felt weightless for a moment. He closed his eyes and heard the flame flapping like a little sail in his ear, the sound reminding him of something he couldn't place – a memory that lipped the edge of his mind but didn't follow through to the front of his head. There was a separation between the sound and the recollection. He saw the mechanics of waiting for it.

The idea hit him that he wasn't responsible for the way his mind worked, that his thoughts had their own course, their own impetus and life, and he was simply a monitor standing by to display them. The notion frightened him; it wasn't the way he usually perceived things, and he pushed it aside. His thoughts were what made him an individual, he told himself. He was at the helm. He was his own man. This was just one of those moments he labeled as strange, and he moved on from it.

He opened his eyes. The space was darker now, the flame at his ear providing half the light, matching the small lamp by his feet.

"I'm feeling some warmth now," he said, trying to gauge how close the flame was to his head by the reflection in the window.

"You're almost there, a couple more minutes."

He could hear her rummaging through something in the back. He stared straight ahead on his side, the lights from town isolated across the water. He played with the illusion that the houseboat was stationary on the black bay and that the distant lights were tilting, that all the land was swaying while he remained motionless.

"Did you ever think there would be times you might forget?" His voice boomed, rumbling through the couch and the walls.

"What?" She emerged from the back with a small wooden trunk in her arms.

"When you were a kid, didn't it seem like you would remember everything, every day? It never crossed my mind that I would forget things, you know what I mean?"

"What things?" She sat on the corner of the table and opened the box in her lap.

"Well, I don't know. That's what I'm saying, I don't remember . . . I know I've forgotten things, little things. I have these vivid memories surrounded by vague ones, made-up ones . . ."

"Made-up?"

"Well, fantasies, things I must've imagined happened."

"Like what?"

"I don't know, dreams maybe. Maybe they're dreams."

"And you believe them?"

"I guess I do, yeah."

"You want them to be part of you."

"Yeah . . ."

"You want to create yourself . . ."

"I don't know if that's quite it, but . . ."

"You want to credit your own efforts, take risks."

She put the box down and knelt by him again.

"You're ready," she said, pulling the burning stub from his ear. She blew it out, sending the rank smoke over him with her breath.

He sat up and faced her in the low light, her eyes level with his chest, the smoking nub of the ear cone between them in her hands. She was posed before him, a stalled frame, pursed. He gripped her by the shoulders and pulled her against him, mashing a kiss on her mouth. He pulled her tight, wrapping himself around her and pried at her lips, forcing his tongue into her. Then he stopped, feeling her body rigid, inanimate, her eyes open.

She looked at him silent, allowing him to recover his arms, then stood up, still holding the crushed butt of the ear cone in her hand.

"I'm sorry," he said.

She stepped to the sink, jerked a drawer open, and began digging through it.

"You think this is a joke?" she said.

"What? No." He feared suddenly.

She walked back with a fillet knife in her hand.

"You need to see something!" she said.

"What are you doing, see what?" He scrambled away from her, bracing himself.

"You need to see!" She sliced open the charred knob of the cone she was still carrying and exposed the earwax inside its core.

"Look!" she said, unfolding the layers in his face, fondling the orange-gold resin with her fingers. "That was all in your head!" Her eyes glinted. "Look at that!"

His heart lurched. He was speechless.

She held the splayed plug of wax in front of him a moment longer, watching him, then set it on the table by the small trunk.

"Now you do the other ear," she said, preparing the second cone, pushing it through the fresh sheet of foil with a practiced command.

He tried to collect himself, climbing down from his perch on the back of the couch.

"One's good for now . . ." His blood crashed through him.

"No. You have to do both ears, you can't do *one,* you have to do *both.* The balance is crucial, it has to be equal!"

She gestured with the knife, pointing the skinny blade to both sides of his head, wielding the new cone in her other hand.

Her voice changed. "You lie back down now. Lie down. We do the other ear now." She crowded over him, and he rolled to his side beneath her, his face against the back of the couch.

"There," she said, slipping the tapered cylinder into his ear, the knife handle rubbing his neck as she adjusted the tube. Her body was close, her breasts brushing his shoulder.

"You hold it there while I light it."

He did what she told him.

She lit the end and stood up, the knife glancing under the foil that draped his head.

"Now keep it upright. Don't move around," she said, her voice resuming its original pitch.

She picked up his wax and the singed remnants of parchment from the table and set it all carefully in the box.

"You're on your way," she said, shutting the lid. She lifted the trunk like an infant and carried it to the back of the boat, each step resounding in his ears.

Blinkers

"You must listen to my idea, angel," Gunilla said at the kitchen doorway.

Hermann wedged the heel of his knee-high riding boot into the crotch of an antique bootjack and grunted as he pulled his foot out.

"Yes, you keep saying, tell me," he said, exhaling and setting the boots neatly beside the small bench in the mudroom.

"You have to envision it . . ." she said.

"Yes, yes."

He sat on the bench in his jodhpurs and socked feet, going through his evening routine of cleaning his boots after his ride. He wiped the mud and salt off with a rag and gently worked the slick leather with a natural sponge, lathering it with water and a glycerin bar.

"So you are envisioning it?" Gunilla asked, a trace of her Swedish upbringing in her voice.

"How can I be envisioning it? You have said nothing!"

"I am going to tell you," she went on. "Imagine now: It is spring, you must picture it – it is spring, there are blooms and birds, the bees are pollinating, maybe a little breeze – "

"This is the wedding you are talking about, yes?" he interrupted.

"Yes, let me continue. It will all be revealed."

"Continue with it," he said, going back to his boots with the sponge.

"There is maybe a little breeze, the bulbs are opening up, and you look at the nature and the trees of the park, you see a long procession of gleaming carriages pulled by teams of horses making their way through the field toward the hills. Behind them are riders, maybe one hundred, two by two, every one in black tie and gowns. The bridesmaids are sidesaddle and they wear hats; they move at a slow walk from the field into the trees. Shadows sprinkle the coaches and the horses and they climb the hill toward the lake . . ."

"Who is in the coaches?" Hermann asked, looking up at her.

"Our family, darling. Our relatives from the old country."

"And we are in a coach?"

"We will be horseback . . . We will be wed *horseback* at the edge of the lake!"

She spoke triumphantly, holding her arms out, and leaned down to kiss his rough cheek.

"I am very grubby, darling," he said, leaning away from her.

"Oh, I don't care about that."

She sat next to him on the bench and pulled him close. "It will be so beautiful. Can't you just see it? Won't it be fantastic?"

"Yes, fantastic."

"It will be beautiful," she said.

He pushed two wooden shoe trees into his boots and inspected them again as he set them down, shrinking his mouth to a short horizontal line of satisfaction. He stood stiffly and walked into the kitchen, stepping into his sandals by the coatrack, and continued toward the bedroom to clean up before supper.

Gunilla sat alone on the bench, listening to him walk down the hall. She looked out the small window of the mudroom at the gray sky above the wet eucalyptus trees that rimmed their property. She longed for sun knowing the rains were coming.

The groundsman, Emiliano, was feeding Hermann's warmblood gelding in the paddock at the bottom of the hill. Gunilla could see his sticklike body from the window, pushing the hay cart to the next pen of eager horses, their heads over the fence in anticipation of the alfalfa. She watched as he threw the flakes into the feeders, and she smiled. She loved to watch the horses eat; she knew it was when they were happiest.

Gunilla had never been married. She was forty-six now and felt she looked it, even though her friends insisted otherwise. She never would have believed as a girl that she would be unwed and childless at this age – it was a blight, as she saw it, that she wished had been righted before her mother passed away ten years before.

She had gone through the whirlwind of her younger sister's wedding the previous summer, organizing the affair. She felt she had taken on their mother's role in the ordeal, hoping that in some way her spirit might see her youngest daughter be a bride through her eyes.

But now it was her own marriage, and the significance of the event had become a neurosis that surprised her. She saw a hint of the absurd in the sentimentality that came up in her head. She was embarrassed by it and tried to focus on the planning. Busying herself on logistics was a good distraction.

She clasped her long hands together on her lap, glancing down at the veins that stood up on the backs. She rubbed her unpainted nails, feeling a strength in them that she remembered in her mother's hands; a grace and dignity in their natural form that she attributed to heredity more than grooming. The association brought a slight clog to her throat, and she stood quickly, then walked into the kitchen to finish preparing supper.

★　　★　　★

"I do not think this is maybe the best idea," Hermann said at the table.

"What, darling?"

"These carriages and relatives, I do not think that would be the best thing."

"Why not? I thought you would love the idea – you don't love the idea? The horses and coaches?"

"I think we should maybe keep it simple," he said, dabbing his mouth with a linen napkin. "It should be easy and quiet . . . A small ceremony. Don't you think a nice small ceremony would be pleasant, something quiet?"

"It will be quiet, darling. We will be in the park, with the breeze wafting off the lake; it will be remote and peaceful . . ."

"I don't think we should make such a spectacle of it is what I am saying, 'Nilla. It's already enough to bring our relatives over, but then to have everyone mount horses and climb into carriages . . . It's excessive."

"Excessive! This is our wedding. It must be unforgettable. Don't you want it to be unforgettable?"

"Yes. Of course, but . . ." He took a sip of his white wine, pushing his chair back from the table to stretch his legs. "Oh, make it how you want. We will do whatever you want. You should be happy with it."

Gunilla went to work setting everything up for the May fifteenth date. She utilized her sister's help to make up the invitations and do the catering while Hermann's secretary organized the travel arrangements and hotel accommodations for their relatives flying in from Germany and Sweden. But most important, she called upon Emiliano, the young groundsman and stable hand, to muster the carriages and teamsters. She explained as best she could the importance of the coaches that were imperative to her plan.

Most of their friends were avid equestrians and members of the saddle club situated at the base of the park, where the ceremony would take place. Gunilla requested in their local invitations that they bring their own horses for the excursion.

Things were coming together swimmingly except that no one owned sidesaddles. The Parkinsons had two turn-of-the-century museum pieces in their den, but they certainly would not have anyone ride them. Emiliano had no luck with his sources, aside from finding one antique hanging on the wall of a used-tack shop – but the proprietor wouldn't rent it out, and Emiliano noted that it probably would have disintegrated if it were put on a horse.

Gunilla stewed over the problem.

"But the gowns and the hats, the bridesmaids! They can't be in riding pants or slacks, Hermann, they can't!" she cried to him in bed.

"We will work something out, darling. It will all be fine."

Gunilla personally called and explained the change to all of the bridesmaids, who were relieved, since none of them had ever ridden sidesaddle before anyway.

After the New Year, the RSVPs began coming in and by the cutoff date of March thirtieth, out of the one hundred fifty invited, ninety-eight confirmed. Gunilla was happy, and she relaxed for the first time in the months of preparation.

Emiliano had his own troubles. He told Gunilla that everything was set with the carriages, but in fact, he could not find any. He drove the worn-out Willy's truck all over the county searching. He checked with his backstretch acquaintances at the racetrack, the local ranchers, and some old farmers. He looked into horse-training facilities and the polo club, but all he found was one buggy and an old buckboard. He knew she had entrusted him with the duty, and he felt his job was on the line.

He finally thought of the fairgrounds, where he found an old man who drove the horse-drawn shuttle for the fair. He had two rubber-wheeled tour wagons with fringed yellow canopies. Long bench seats faced each other running the length of each wagon, which could hold sixteen people. It was the best Emiliano could find, and he explained to the teamster in his most formal English that money was no object, hoping he would agree to lease out his services for the wedding.

"It's off-season for me, you understand, son . . ." the

143

old man told him, oiling harness in a small dark shed behind the barns. Emiliano could barely make out his face, only hear his deep voice and see the movement of his arms handling the harness. "I've got my mares turned out in the off-season; they don't get legged up till July for the fair."

"I understand, sir," Emiliano said, trying to focus on the man. "This is very important. We will pay you for the day. It is for only one day, and it would mean the world to my patrons. You are my only hope – you will be the savior if you can do this!"

"Well, I'd have to have my son drive the other team. I ain't gonna have any greenhorn drivin' my mares."

"That would be exactly right," Emiliano said.

"I need things done a certain way, savvy?"

"I understand, sir."

"The savior, huh?" The old man laughed.

"Yes, sir."

Emiliano was relieved, and he confirmed with Gunilla that the carriages were in order, including that he and his younger cousin, Adolfo, a part-time helper, would ride along with the procession as outriders in case of any mishaps. Time restraints kept her from seeing the carriages herself before the event, and so she had to trust that Emiliano had made the right decision. But she felt he had, and she commended him for his good work.

★　　★　　★

Record-breaking heat came on the day of the wedding.

Gunilla had worried that the early spring showers and dismal grayness that were prevalent in the weeks leading up would foul the event, but the sky cleared the day before and the sun leapt out in the morning, baking down on the damp earth and late-winter grass. Insects were rampant and flitted through the wildflowers and pink crab-apple blossoms that lined the drive from the main road to the saddle-club parking area, where the large group of people and horses were assembled.

The lot was filled with new sport-utility vehicles and shiny trucks towing aluminum trailers, staggered in rows with their loading ramps down and the horses tied to the sides switching their tails at the fresh life of flies in the air. Rental vans and metallic sedans reflected the sun as the old family members from abroad climbed out and squinted, fanning their pallid faces with hats and hotel leaflets in the morning heat. They mumbled sternly in German and Swedish, trying to find someone in charge. The two fair wagons were staged near the entry to the lot, hooked up and waiting with a team of large gray Percheron mares harnessed to the old teamster's wagon and a pair of Belgian draft mules hooked to his son's. The two men sat tensely in their rented suits holding the driving lines and talked quietly while their animals shook their heads and rubbed against each other in the stillness.

The park loomed beyond the clubhouse courtyard, with

giant eucalyptus and oak trees that climbed to the top ridge of the small mountain, mimicking its line against the sky that glared pale and cloudless over the large congregation below.

The women laughed and kissed each other's cheeks, smiling and admiring the horses, complimenting one another's hats while the men looked at each other's new saddles and trailers, discussing farrier science and inspecting the feet of their mounts. The young daughters were bored and pretty, trying to keep their dresses clean, sipping soda on their monogrammed tack trunks while the sons chased lizards or anything else they might kill. The minister mingled with the group in his robes, smiling serenely. The morning was bright and clear and held promise in the unforeseen warmth of the day.

Emiliano and Adolfo jogged their common, quiet horses from the barns toward the clubhouse, laughing and teasing in Spanish at the silly suits they wore. Adolfo thought it hilarious that they should be paid to look so foolish, and Emiliano reminded him to be tactful around the guests.

The club members mounted their horses and adjusted their clothes while the minister and grim foreigners reluctantly climbed aboard the two wagons, segregating themselves: German in one and Swedish in the other. The two Mexican outriders arrived and surveyed the huge group, moving among them and smiling professionally as the last of the Swedes hoisted themselves into the mule wagon.

Everyone was ready and, at the signal from the old

teamster, the two gray draft mares leaned into their collars, and led the train into the field toward the park.

The long procession was spectacular with the yellow canopied wagons at the head followed by the seventy riders, two abreast. The spectrum of colors in the horses – from the dappled gray mares through the sorrels, bays and browns, blacks, paints, and duns – complemented the array of hats, blouses, and jackets worn by the riders. The pace was slow and orderly, in a parade that caught the light and richness of the spring morning and shone in the field against the dark grass.

The bride and groom waited at the mouth of the fire-road trail, watching from their horses as the train of riders neared. Hermann, in his tailed tuxedo and black riding boots, sat stoically beside the bride, his wide-blazed warmblood gelding arching its thick neck and collecting its head in classical dressage posture.

Gunilla felt light-headed and blamed it on the heat. Her face was flushed and sticky with makeup as she sat her bay Thoroughbred and flourished her skirts to ventilate the heavy white gown. She then tucked them back under her and tried to get comfortable in her English saddle.

"I didn't expect this heat," she said, embarrassed by the sweat that tingled on her forehead.

Hermann smiled, concentrating on his horse, who grew uneasy from the approaching sounds of harnesses and wheels.

A sudden horrible look took over Gunilla's face.

"They're not coaches, Hermann!" she yelled. "They're not coaches or carriages, they're *wagons!*"

"It's lovely, darling. It looks lovely," he said, correcting his gelding who side-passed and salivated, tensing its hocks and prancing as the first wagon went by them.

"My God, and mules! My family is being drawn by mules!"

"Oh, it's all right, darling."

"Mules, Hermann! I never would have . . . How could Emilio have done this?"

"Never mind. It's Emiliano, but never mind, there's nothing to be done about it now, is there?"

"I can't believe he could do this."

"Let it go, please. Everything is grand. It is wonderful, look! Look at your idea. Here it is, 'Nilla, look at it!"

She struggled to smile as the expectant faces of the parade focused on her. Her eyelids twitched, and her lips stuck to her teeth. She saw her Swedish aunts and uncles in the second wagon and her father, all craning their old heads stiffly to look upon her. Her young sister and her husband followed horseback and, close behind, the ten bridesmaids, pink-cheeked and emotional, in their pale yellow dresses, contained themselves as best they could but inadvertently squeezed their mounts into a jig. The Parkinsons were on their flashy overo paints, and the Olsens followed wearing identical beige outfits. The Ingerlechts stretched their necks out like geese, matching the western-pleasure quarter horses they rode.

She recognized every face down the line, every smiling face that winked or nodded or laughed, and she missed her mother. She wished she was there to see it. To see her.

"You see, darling, it's wonderful," Hermann said, noticing her wet eyes.

"Yes, it is quite lovely," she laughed out, congested and sniffling.

She wiped her eyes and nose and regained her composure as the two of them filed in behind the last horses and followed the train into the woods.

The temperature rose.

The shade of the madrone and eucalyptus that had initially provided some relief from the direct sun now held a mustiness, and the air became stagnant, trapping the humidity in the branches. The air was stifling, and by eleven o'clock, it was suffocating – ninety-five degrees and still.

The Percheron mares were in a full sweat, their gray coats dark along their necks and flanks, wet through to their black skin. They struggled with the weight of the German relatives and the heavy steel-framed wagon as they led the procession, unseen by the bride and groom who were last in the long line.

The horses and people were smothered by the freakish

heat; it steamed off the animals and built inside the formal clothing of the riders. The conversations subsided,
and the group marched quietly as the incline of the fire
road increased and switchbacked up the mountain. The
gray mares and giant mules blew hard and lathered from
the friction of their harnesses, foaming white under the
leather straps and collars. They were out of condition and
unprepared for the hard climb; they grew fearful and balked
from the soreness in their necks. But the teamsters drove
them on, cursing the bride and groom under their breath
and resenting the unhappy load of foreigners that weighed
them down. The trail became narrower and still steeper.
The teams clambered over rocks and boulders that had
been loosed by the recent rains, torquing the front axles of
the wagons and violently swinging the heavy steel tongues
against the horses' legs as they hunkered from the strain. The
old Germans swayed under the canopy, bracing themselves,
and muttered angrily at the jerky ride, exclaiming that they
would rather be walking. Similar sentiment went through
the second wagon as the thin Swedes rocked from the jarring
ascent, squaring their feet for balance and clutching the side
rails of the wagon.

Adolfo, impervious to the heat, rode beside the ten
bridesmaids, who were now red-faced with sweat. He
moved smugly from one to the other under the pretense
of protector, flirting blatantly and showing off in the saddle,
but they ignored him. The couples who followed behind

were amused by the scene, but only briefly before the heat struck them again, forcing them to loosen their collars as they rode on.

The even walking pace broke down to a staggered stop-and-go through the trees as the long train backed up and bunched in the tight turns of the trail, waiting on the wagons to make their slow snaking course out of sight.

"Emilio!" Gunilla called, seeing him make his way back beside the line of riders.

"It's Emiliano, darling," Hermann said quietly. "You're not going to be cross with him now, 'Nilla?"

"No, I'm not going to be cross with him," she said.

Emiliano paralleled the procession that was now at another standstill, and he sidled his horse to the bride's.

"Yes, ma'am?"

"Why do we continue to stop? Can we not keep an easy walk?" she asked him.

"It's the carriages, ma'am, they have difficulty with the turns. I do not think they are ever in the hills maybe."

Gunilla looked sharply at Hermann on the word *carriages*, then back at Emiliano.

"I won't go into it now," she said, "but did you not tell me there would be – "

"Gunilla!" Hermann interrupted her. "Please, darling."

"Well, see if you can get the *carriages* under way. We have a time frame, and it's dreadfully hot back here."

"Yes, ma'am," Emiliano said, and he kicked his stock

horse into a trot, passing the stopped couples on their right as he made his way toward the front of the procession.

"Does he not know the difference between a carriage and a wagon?" Gunilla asked, watching Emiliano disappear around the bend in the trail.

"I suppose not, dear, but please, you should not be thinking of these things now. We are almost there," Hermann said, schooling his horse again to contain its high action in showring form.

Emiliano rode along the narrow trail, passing the standing horses and couples. The people were strangers to him, but he recognized most of the horses from feeding and mucking stalls at the boarding stables.

"Pardon me, pardon me," he called out as he went, trotting his horse between the shale rock wall on his right and the many riders to his left who moved out of his way to the edge of the trail. He could see broken views through the oak and bay branches of the field and saddle club far below, the riding arena, and various pens. They had come a long way up, and the heat had increased. He grew concerned with the halt in the procession, they were near the turn to the lake. It should have been moving again by now, he thought, and his pace became more urgent, as though he were responsible for the delay.

"What's the holdup?" a man's voice called after Emiliano as he trotted past. He had no answer for him, but he feared then that something was wrong. He pretended not to hear and continued up the hill. The trail curved right again, and he saw the bridesmaids in their yellow dresses and the mule wagon all stopped up ahead. There was a cleft in the hills where the fire road went through the pass to the lake, and Emiliano saw that the first wagon was off to the left side. He could only see the back of it, as the driver and Percheron team were obscured by branches.

Then he heard the old teamster yelling.

Emiliano felt the heat beat into him as adrenaline climbed quickly through his neck and temples. Adolfo's horse was walking loose in the trail, and the teamster's son was waving his arms wildly from the mule wagon. A bridesmaid screamed, and the old relatives were trying to climb out of the front wagon.

One of the big mares was down.

He kicked his horse into a lope, passing the bridesmaids and mule wagon, and then skidded up to the yelling teamster.

The two-thousand-pound mare was stretched out stiff on her side, still hooked to the wagon and kicking her hind legs spastically against the tongue and doubletree. Adolfo was on foot in the thick madrone branches in front of them, trying to hold the head of the standing mare who scrambled and side-passed, blowing low terrified groans as she looked beyond her blinkers to her thrashing partner on the ground. Emiliano jumped from his horse and ran to the fallen mare.

"Unhook the traces! Goddamnit, unhook her traces!" the old man yelled from the seat, pulling back on the lines.

The wagon began creeping backward down the trail, and the Germans panicked trying to climb out.

"Block the wheels! Get these people off!" the man yelled.

The wagon continued to roll backward, dragging the downed mare over the rocks. Adolfo tried to hold the standing mare, but the grade and weight were too much. She spooked and swung away, jackknifing the front axle and stretching the lines, pulling against the weight of her collapsed partner. She squatted and reared, lifting Adolfo off the ground with her giant neck as the tug straps dug into her hip. The teamster leapt to the ground as the Germans piled out. The back wheels caught up in the rocks and stopped rolling, but the standing mare continued to fight as the fallen horse convulsed in the dirt.

"She's havin' a heart attack!" the old man screamed, trying to free the dying animal from the wagon, unhooking the tug straps and neck yoke, then pulling the bridle from her head.

"Unhook the tugs!" he yelled, pointing to the other mare.

Emiliano jumped into the mess of leather lines and straps between the horses and unsnapped the tugs from the doubletree.

"She's loose!" he yelled to his cousin, who still had her

by the head, and Adolfo pulled the standing mare free of the wagon.

Emiliano and the old man worked quickly, stripping the harness off the shuddering horse on the ground.

"Watch her feet!" the teamster yelled as she thrashed again in agony. They yanked the bellyband loose, then the quarter-straps, and unbuckled the hames and collar from around her neck. She let out air that popped mucus from her nostrils and rushed with the sound of wind, rasping at once high-pitched and guttural.

The teamster's son joined them from the mule wagon, and the three pulled the sweat-soaked harness from her back. They used their weight together to free the holdback strap from under her, pulling until it ripped loose, and they dropped it all in a heap on the rocks.

Emiliano stood above the pile of leather, oil and sweat on his hands. He froze, watching as the father and son rushed back to the animal, the old man grabbing at the mare's jaw, searching for a pulse. He shook his head and yelled her name. More of the horrible wind came from her nostrils and pale mouth as her eyes spun white and dead. The son clasped his hands in a double fist and swung from high over his head a hard blow that thudded hollow on her ribs. Her lips shrank back, and Emiliano could see her long, ridged teeth. He saw the dust blow up around her mouth from the air that only left her. The son swung again, and the flesh of her giant barrel absorbed the impact. He swung again. A twitch rippled through her mass. Then she was still.

The old man stopped his son from swinging again.

Emiliano stared at the backs of the two men kneeling over the dark body, disbelief holding him motionless. He saw the horrified faces of the relatives huddled in a mob near the mule wagon. Most of the bridesmaids had dismounted and were comforting one another. Some of the men from the procession were on foot as well and looked on, their wives still mounted and turned away.

Suddenly the distressed call of the surviving mare cut the quiet, braying through the trees and echoing off the rocks. Adolfo still held her on the other side of the empty wagon. She swung her head wildly, crying openmouthed. She looked to where the dead horse had stood, then up the trail. She pitched around to see behind her, not connecting the carcass on the ground with the loss. She screamed and wheeled, dragging Adolfo with her as she spun in search of her companion who had inexplicably vanished.

Emiliano could only think of the bride and groom. He realized they were so far back in the line of people that they would not have witnessed the tragedy. He knew he would have to get the procession moving again before the word got to them. He picked up the silver-capped hames at his feet and dragged the tangled harness out of the trail. He threw the giant knot of leather and buckles into the empty wagon and dropped the dirty collar on top.

He could see the lake through the cleft in the hills, no more than two hundred yards away.

"We are very close, everyone!" he yelled to the bridesmaids and old relatives with sudden enthusiasm. "The lake is right ahead!" he said, smiling. "We can walk. It is very close. You see the water?"

They looked at him vacantly, then talked low to each other, translating what he had said. The bridesmaids stared blankly down the trail.

"Everyone get back on your horses, please!" he said, taking control of the stunned onlookers, and they slowly began moving.

Emiliano went to the old teamster, who still knelt over the dead mare. The son stepped away, relieving Adolfo of wrangling the other horse, who continued to fret and paw at the ground.

"We must cover her somehow," Emiliano said, kneeling beside the man.

"She's my best mare," the old man said, not looking up.

"We will pay you . . ."

"I broke her to drive as a four-year-old."

"I am so sorry."

"Never had a lame day in her life."

"We will, of course, pay, but . . ." The old man looked at him, and anger quivered in his eyes. The sudden proximity felt invasive, and Emiliano stood up.

"If I'd known how rough this deal was gonna be, I'd never agreed to it," the old man said from his knees. "These mares aren't used to pullin' hills. When they were young, they'd pull a house down, but they work in the flat now, runnin' the shuttle from the parking lot to the palladium. They ain't used to work like this! Hell, them mules are barely holdin' up!"

"I understand," Emiliano said, eager to hide the body from the guests, but, more important, from the bride and groom.

"This goddamned heat and all these freakin' people don't do us sickum either – all for this, for this *wedding*. Lose my best damn mare for this? Where are those people? I've never even talked to those people."

"Please, can we wait? After the ceremony, please – they must have the day – "

"What in Sam Hill do you think this is, some kinda *inconvenience*?" the man yelled, standing up. "I got a dead horse on the ground and her partner over there goin' into shock 'cause she's never been apart from her! Those mares eat, shit, and sleep like they're hooked together in a hitch! They graze out in pasture side by side, no more than two feet from each other! I've lost them both. She'll never get past this. You don't know about these teams, son – you break up a lifetime together like that – you never get 'em back. You lose one, you lose the other."

The old man pulled his awkward jacket off and threw

it disgustedly on the body of the mare, then walked away to join his son. Emiliano watched the men try to comfort the other horse, touching her shoulders on either side, then leading her away from the wagon and into the trees.

Adolfo had caught their two stock horses and led them over to the jackknifed wagon as Emiliano hastily gathered branches and dead limbs from the trail edge and dragged them back. He quickly covered the carcass with the debris and positioned Adolfo and the two horses beside the unsightly body.

The procession regained order and continued, though slowly and with uncertainty. The old relatives, abandoning the wagons, passed on foot. They bowed their heads and quietly went on toward the lake, Swedes and Germans together. The bridesmaids remounted and rode by, glancing quickly at the two Mexican men who stood smiling with their docile mounts, blocking the view of the dead mare. The couples whispered as they passed, but most were unclear on what had happened. They tried to look beyond Emiliano and Adolfo, but the two men had managed to hide everything.

The heat took over again, and as the long train of riders went by, fewer and fewer had knowledge of the accident until the bride and groom finally appeared around the turn in the narrow trail, completely ignorant of the event.

"Where is everyone?" Gunilla asked Emiliano, motioning toward the vacated wagons.

"They decided to walk, ma'am," he said, repositioning his horse to hide the corpse as she went past. "They are all at the lake waiting. It is very close," he said, diverting her attention to the glint of water ahead of them.

She and Hermann both looked straight ahead as the train passed through the cleft in the hills, Hermann concentrating on his gelding, who snorted and tensed as he caught scent of the dead mare. The two Mexican men moved their horses together to assure no sight of the body was possible, and the bride and groom rode through the natural gateway to the lake without noticing.

The fire road opened up beyond the break in the hills, the sun shining hard on the dark water, and the quiet congregation parted to form an aisle.

"It is very nearly how you envisioned it, yes?" Hermann asked.

"Yes, darling. Yes, it is," Gunilla answered him.

A long, resonating wail of a horse came from the woods behind the bride and groom as they marched in the open field between the many couples and family members. Gunilla turned her head at the woeful sound, but quickly disregarded it and smiled again for her family and guests as the ceremony finally began.

Already Gone

"Can I get you something? Some peanuts or something?"

"No, I've got to run," she says, leaning toward the door.

"You just got here."

"I know. I only stopped to say hi, that's all."

He stands up from the fire he's lit in the stove and walks around the sofa bed that fills most of his studio apartment. He feels the air grow cooler as he catches up behind her at the door and wraps his arms around her shoulders, holding her back against his chest. They rock slightly, looking out the small window in the door at the dusk light outside, his cheek on hers, his chin rubbing her neck. The automatic darkness-sensing lamp at the corner of his house tries to make up its mind, fluttering coldly in pale green flashes across the muddy driveway.

"It's strange light," she says.

She hasn't taken her jacket off, and he feels her voice is too far away for how close he's holding her. He feels she's allowing him to hold her. There's some comfort in it, but he knows if he loosens his grip, she'll slip out and be gone down the driveway before he can say her name.

"Which light?" he asks.

"The light outside!"

"No, I know, but you mean the sky or that . . . that flickering?" He loosens his hands to make a flashing movement, and she responds to the letup, inching away from him before he gently pulls her back close.

"The flickering light," she says, again giving in to his arms around her.

Her visits are getting shorter. He's tried to tell her on the phone that it drives him crazy the way she says hello and good-bye within minutes. She's argued that it's better than not stopping by at all, and this worries him. He doesn't know which is better; he wants another option. He begins seeing her subtle leans toward the door as a cue to prove himself to her, that each visit is a new trial. The shorter her visits become, the more he tries to convince her. He feels if he can keep her engaged, she might see his devotion. It isn't solely sexual; they have slept together, they've been with each other for months. Six months, he thinks. He isn't sure, many months he knows. It's more that he wants her to crave his touch, that she might long for him.

"That light doesn't level out until it's dark," he says.

"It's got a sensor on it?" she asks, without real question or interest, only movement toward the door.

He's only been with women that are simpler than her, stepping up to them with decisive action and asserting himself, taking control and prevailing by his tactics, as he sees it. But she's different, she's delicate in a way that makes him see his usual manner as brutish. There's no fooling her with manliness or rash stunts of passion; she doesn't fall for any of his posturing. She holds the power to knock the bottom out of any technique a man might have.

"Yeah, there's a light sensor on it," he says.

"I've really got to go, babe," she says, turning herself within his arms to face him.

He knows she has to go, that she's inherently uneasy. He knows he's attracted to her as a result, and he kisses her. He kisses her squarely, and she smiles through it, against his mouth, making light of the contact he hopes might sway her to stay. She sees an opportunity to break free in the uncertain separation she has caused. She smiles at arm's length like a sibling at a bus station, and steps out the door.

He could leave it at that. He could be the one waving from his doorway while she tromps across the muddy cul-de-sac in her bulky shoes. He can see himself being that man, letting her go as if they've reached a level of trust in one another, as if they are safe in their own hearts.

The thought flies through him in the time of a drip falling from the corrugated fiberglass awning to the concrete slab of his front porch. He imagines waiting, listening to the last of her tire sound down his rutted driveway between the fig trees and the woodshed. He imagines being left with the emptiness of the view and the seasonal roar of oblivious toads in the drainage ditch, and he steps out after her, squishing into the creamy mud.

Her car is nosed away from his house, positioned for an easy exit, and she's already inside with the motor running. He's afraid of frightening her. He sees the back of her head that reveals nothing of her nature. She could be eighteen from the back, he thinks, her straight light hair suggesting a girl he's maybe dreamed of. He feels he should break into song or scream her name. He walks with exaggerated movements, swinging his arms and swaying his body to catch her attention in the mirrors – hoping to not startle her when he appears at her side window in the dim light.

She doesn't see his clownish walk. She puts the car in gear and starts off, forcing him to run and hit the trunk with his palm to stop her.

"Jesus! You scared me," she says, rolling the window down half-mast.

"I'm sorry . . . you were taking off . . ." He hasn't planned anything beyond that, stopping her is the extent of his thought. The courage he mustered at his doorway, the vision he'd had of coming up next to her, the imaginary turning point in his head, is all horribly in the past for him.

"So . . . what's up?" she asks, looking up at him, her face framed by the window gap.

"I don't want you to leave," he says.

She doesn't answer.

He surprises himself with the statement, a prickle of confidence rising within him looking down at her in the car. He feels her impending departure hanging on his actions, his silence holding her in the driveway.

"I'll come back, you know," she says.

He wants to tell her that she makes him a man, but that seems ridiculous. He wants to tell her how afraid he is, that he wants to mature and abandon rituals that are outmoded or false to his nature. He wants her to see his heart and blood, the driving storm of his interior, the loneliness that pushes him to be the man for her. He wants her to understand his aloneness.

"Are you okay?" she asks, a slight concern at the edge of her mouth.

He dives his head through the space of her window, pushing his shoulders against the half-rolled pane as he reaches for her lips and connects in a startled kiss that keeps her eyes open. He feels the glass giving to his weight, and he wants it to break. He wants it to shatter between them and fall to the floorboards as he feels the warmth of her mouth and skin – a sensation beyond sight or focus in his teeth and hers, their tongues alive without words. She rolls the window down, letting him in, eating at him, probing without thought, letting him come inside the car with her, letting him reach his arms and hands, letting him envelop her. She holds him. She pulls at him, licks him. She tastes all of his face and neck, his ears, his hair, succumbing to a shared separateness that has its own life without them. Then suddenly she backs away, pulling up with the same definitive commitment that had welcomed the embrace. She pulls back, leaving him wedged against the door, and looks forward through the windshield. She resets her feet and her bus-stop smile returns.

He backs his torso out and stands straight, looking over her roof to his small house. The corner light has steadied, bugs swarm it in erratic shadows.

"I'm going to go now," she says, still looking forward down the driveway.

He takes a step back and looks at her – the side of her face already gone, her lips and eyes, her hands already down the road. He's still alone, listening to her tires in the ruts fading away to the toads, the smoke climbing sideways from the chimney. She's already gone, and he walks back across the mud to his porch. He wipes his feet and goes inside where the fire he lit is still burning on its own.

Jubilee King

I punched out at five and walked past the tracks behind the mill toward town. The train doesn't come by anymore – all the grain comes in on trucks. We clean it, then reclean it and turn it into whatever feed, laying mash or hog grower, sometimes just the whole grain. I'm still a rebagger, me and five other guys. The boss sees we're fresh out of school, so he doesn't put on too much responsibility. I'm not sure how a guy could work his way up or why he'd want to, going through damaged sacks and restitching them in new bags. It's a summer job I picked up, and that's about it. There's no real interest other than working a little closer to agriculture, which is what I want, I guess. Farming seems like the right thing.

The old man Nat works in the office upstairs with the secretaries. He started at the mill forty years ago or

167

something, doing the same as me, back when the trains still ran. He knows feed, livestock, farming. He's a horse trainer or breeder or both; that's what the guys tell me. I've never really talked to him until today. He asked me to help him dig a hole after work, said he'd give me twenty bucks for a couple hours, so I said all right. It gets dark by eight, but he said we'd leave at six. Summer's about done, and we'll be into the rain soon. I can already feel it coming.

I turned toward the billiard hall on Los Puestos Avenue to burn the hour before Nat would be through with his paperwork in the office. I was beat from working all day, not the work so much as the time put in, and I wished I hadn't agreed to help Nat. Digging was better morning work, but it was twenty bucks.

All six tables were being used when I went in. I got a Sprite and a strip of beef jerky from the counter and went to the red-felt tables in back where we usually play. Julio was there and a couple other guys from work. They had the day off and were already in a money game. None of them looked up from the table. Julio had been there for a while; he likes to run the pot for the games.

"*¿Qué onda?*" I said to him, and we knocked fists like we always do. He's buddies with me now that I'm older, treats me like I'm part of things, but he's still kind of hard. He refuses to speak English even though he understands most of it. We go back and forth. I speak Spanish with my family but talking to Julio is different. He tests me on it, jumping from high-speed slang to crazy English. He feels California is rightfully ours, that we were here and we owned it before anyone else, so we should take pride. He says *we* like it's some army we have, some revolution. My brother's the same way. They always go off about the labor and where California would be without us, as if it were a real thing to put our effort into. I agree with them most of the time; it's the right thing to do – to agree – but working seems more important to me. Wasting everything being mad about it doesn't make sense.

"So, you going to help the old man?" Julio asked, organizing the bills for the pot.

"How'd you know?" I said.

"He asks all the guys."

"What is it, a trench?" I asked him.

"No, we dug down a few feet, then we filled it back up – that was it. Marcelo and Jo Jo helped him too."

They looked up from the red table when they heard their names, and they nodded to me like they hadn't seen me come in.

"Salvador's going to help the old man dig!" Julio says to them in Spanish.

They laughed and went back to the game.

I watched them for a few rounds, trying to figure how I could get out of helping Nat.

"You helped him, too?" I asked Marcelo between shots.

"Yeah."

"The same hole?"

"No, another. There are many."

"What's he digging for?"

"I don't know. He paid me. That's all I know."

He shrugged and smiled, then did his usual switch from the simple guy he always is, to the hard-core player that he becomes on the table. His face gets brutal, and the cue does what he wants. Nobody beats Marcelo.

I kept checking the clock at the counter, wondering if I should just bail out on Nat, but at ten to six I started back.

"*¡Buena suerte!*" Julio said, and I heard them all laugh again as I walked away.

The billiard hall was dark, but it was still light outside, and the sun came over the top of the old false-front Chamber of Commerce and real estate buildings across the street. The light cut me in half, leaving my legs in shadow and my head in the sun as I walked back toward the mill.

The work trucks from the housing developments uptown went by me with their Dawson Son's Construction logo on the doors, ten or twelve white trucks that took up the whole road, hauling ass toward the highway. They think they own the place now with all the construction.

I turned off the drag and crossed back over the tracks. Nat's brown pickup was sitting in the same spot it'd been in since that morning. I saw he was already in it, and I jogged over.

"I hope you're not waiting for me," I said when I opened the door.

"No, you're on time, Salvador."

I liked that he called me by my name instead of *amigo* like he calls the rest of the guys.

His cologne hit me right off, coming out of the bench-seat upholstery with all the old men I've known – my grandfather and uncles, all of them have that same spicy ammonia smell that doesn't cover anything up, just mixes with their own odor. I had never been so close to him. I guess he's maybe sixty, but I can't tell. He's one of those men that would look good for his age if he's sixty. He wore a striped snap shirt, pointed Western boots, and a straw hat that was creased up like the ones on those black-and-white TV cowboys from the fifties. His mustache sits out away from his face and hides his teeth when he talks.

"Well, I appreciate this, Salvador," he said, starting the truck.

"No trouble," I said, wondering how much trouble it might be.

We pulled out and got on the frontage road heading north toward the valley. I didn't know where we were going. I thought it would be close since the sun was going down, but he drove the straight road out of town like we would be on it for a while, settling into the seat without any hurry on the gas pedal.

"So, what're you, nineteen?" he asked.

"Twenty," I told him.

"What do you think of the work?"

"At the mill? . . . It's good, I guess."

"You don't have an accent. You speak Spanish?"

"A little. Just to my mother," I told him.

He nodded and checked his mirror. "The other boys don't speak much English," he said.

I knew they didn't speak much to *him,* but I didn't say anything.

The land changes past the tract homes and condos on the outskirts. It's just rye fields and orchard-grass pastures spread out to the hills that surround the valley. All the vegetable farmland and almond orchards are farther north.

We didn't say anything for a while, just drove like it was his normal commute home. I thought he might ask about my family or school or any of those usual questions, but he didn't and I worried about how far we were going and the sun going down. It didn't make sense to be digging in the dark.

"How far are we going?" I asked him.

"A little ways. You got a date?"

"No, it's just getting dark."

He didn't answer, and I looked out my side window at the fields going by. Two crows were perched on a Dawson Son's Construction sign, and I followed them, turning in the seat as we passed. I saw two shovels in the bed of the truck, and I relaxed a little.

"This used to all be sheep and cattle," he said as I turned back to face forward. "It's just gettin' eaten up by all this."

He nodded toward the Dawson sign we had passed, and I gathered what he meant.

"We used to run cattle through here when I was your age. This was all summer pasture."

I looked out at the dry yellow hills, and I couldn't really picture it. I couldn't imagine him being my age.

"We owned all of this. My family. I bet you didn't know that."

"No, sir," I said.

"It's probably hard to imagine how that might've been. Just horses. Cattle . . . I bet you can't picture that."

"I can picture it," I said, and in some ways I could. I remembered my uncle's ranch in Mexico that I visited when I was twelve. It was just animals and people – no machines.

"You know about horses? Some Mexicans are good horsemen – you ever worked with horses?"

"I have ridden some," I told him.

"What's that, like a pony ride or something?" he said as if I was a little boy.

"My uncle has horses," I told him.

"It's all about horses . . . It's all about the horses."

His voice went soft, and I could hear something stir up in him, something that maybe my uncle would understand.

I knew how the animals were used and worked. My uncle depended on them, never treating them like pets, and Nat seemed to come from the same camp.

"People lose sense of what got it started out here . . ." he said. "They forget."

We slowed for a right turn, and he cranked the steering wheel hand over hand, then accelerated, letting the wheel spin back as we straightened out and went east toward the hills. The last of the sun was behind us and lit up the rye-grass on either side.

"It's just business anymore . . ." he said. "You've got these high-roller Thoroughbred breeders with more money than God, they're thinkin' business profit, and they got some incorrect pig-eyed colt in front of 'em that looks good on paper, but he's half-brained and can't hold up to his own speed . . . They breed things in, breed things out . . . Don't even get me started on it."

I hadn't got him started, but I got the feeling he wanted me to. I could tell he hadn't talked to anyone in a while – not anyone that spoke English.

"It's blood . . ." he said, getting himself started. "Pedigree, some stud way back that's supposed to justify the mess of flesh they've got on the ground. Sure they're fast, they're all quick as snot, but they're back at the knee or toed-in, they can't eat right, their lungs bleed when they work out, bowed tendons, torn suspensories. They end up being dog food before they're three!"

We went faster as he talked, and I stared at the road that narrowed ahead of us.

"There's certain things you've got to push for in breeding – it all comes down to conformation and temperament. There's no point having a horse if it can't *be* a horse. I love the sport; watching those animals run is like I don't know what, like touching a beautiful woman. But the industry that it's become . . . these man-made creatures . . ."

He stroked his mustache straight down with his palm and rocked in the seat as if the issue was continuing in his head – his foot letting up on the gas pedal, slowing to a crawl. I was afraid to say anything, seeing him stare ahead, slowly wiping his mustache down as if he'd forgotten I was in the truck with him.

The sun had gone, but there was still some light in the sky behind us as we crawled toward the hills. The whole idea of helping him dig seemed far off, like something that was still back at the mill or in the pool hall and not a real event that we were getting closer to. I thought of the guys chuckling at each other, tried to picture them individually in the truck with Nat, driving this same road.

The silence and slow pace made me nervous. We turned again to the right and headed south along the foothills. I looked out my window across the dark fields we had crossed to the pale light above the horizon, and a heavy uneasiness came on me, pressing in my stomach. It was a feeling I remember as a kid when it hit me for the first time that there was no way to get around the night, I was stuck with it, and death became real to me. It was in the light or the dropping temperature, the in-between part without sun where it could almost go either way, and I used to wish it would magically become morning again.

"Everyone's on this quarter-horse ticket!" Nat blurted out, and his right foot responded, flooring the gas and whipping my head back as we accelerated.

"America's horse, they claim . . ." he said, picking up from some unknown place and continuing out loud. "But you trace them back to those foundation sires like Joe Bailey and Steel Dust – they're all Morgans! Or take a horse like Driftwood, his grandsire was a registered Morgan. *That's* the breed, good-minded, hearty. They don't kill themselves dodgin' their own shadow like these others. They're solid. That's what I breed. Morgans."

"What are we doing out here?" I asked, thinking he might be talking to himself.

He stared straight ahead and rocked in the seat again.

"I had this mare," he went on, "she was solid bay, nothing flashy. Broke to drive, worked cattle. She was by a Morgan stud called Jubilee King."

We slowed again as he kept talking, easing down to a rate that I practically could've walked at.

"She had three good fillies, three beautiful babies. And one colt."

We pulled off the road and stopped as if his body knew

where to park the truck and his head had nothing to do with it. He killed the motor and sat still, framed in profile by the dark yellow hillside out his window. His words got quiet.

"She was old, and there were complications with the colt . . . I'd been up checking on her, but you know how they are, they always foal between watches. It was early in the morning, still dark. By the time I got to her she was in bad shape. She'd herniated. I called the vet out."

He paused and looked at the hillside for a second.

"We ended up havin' to put her down. Right there in the foaling pen . . . I talked to her. She kept looking for the colt, she'd lift her head and call to him. I pulled him up next to her so she could smell him. I wrapped towels around him and pushed his nose in to suckle so he'd get the colostrum. I got him to nurse with them both on the ground . . . He wouldn't have made it without that first milk."

I heard something in his voice then that I thought came from a place he really didn't want to get started on. It relaxed me for a second, pulling my attention to him. It was in his voice more than the words, a strange proud tone that seemed more fragile than what he was saying.

"I raised that colt from the moment she died. Milk replacers, creep feed . . . I started losing this place, and I had to sell everything, all the horses, the fillies, the other mares I had, all of 'em. The cattle. It was crazy – selling it all to save the property. It didn't make sense . . . It wasn't enough, even with everything sold, it wasn't enough. It came down to me and this stud colt, and there was no way I could part with him. I hung on to him . . . He's five now, and the best stud I've ever had. It's all him, it's all down to him now that I've lost all this. He's got Jubilee King's stamp on him – the mind and temperament, the heart, the feet, the bone, all of it. You don't come across Jubilee blood out here; you just don't find it. It could turn things around, and I'm not gonna let them keep me from makin' a run at it – even with them trying to kill me off with these committees and boards. They're all against me – they take my land and leave me with one shot to get back on my feet with this horse, and now I can't register him! He's worthless as a stud if I can't register him."

"What're you talking about?" I asked.

"The Morgan Horse Association DNA-types mares now. It used to just blood-type sires. They keep all the samples on record to protect against fraud and verify foals and that. But now they've mandated all *mares* be typed too."

He looked at me hard as though the situation was clear.

"I never drew blood on the mare – the law passed after she died."

We sat quiet, and I tried to put it together.

"I can't prove my colt is out of her or that she was sired by Jubilee King without her blood or a DNA sample . . . That's why we're here. I've talked to the contractors and the attorneys and all those people, but they won't allow me on the land. It's in violation of something, I don't know, so I've got to sneak out here like this."

I knew then what we were digging for, and a sensation like static traveled along my arms.

"It's dark enough now . . ." he said. "I don't want to keep you all night."

The dome light stunned me as he opened his door. He stepped out and swung it shut, slamming me back into the dimness of the cab. I heard him drag the shovels over the tailgate, a long dull scrape and then a metal-on-metal pop as the heads clanked over and swung to the gravel shoulder. I got out, and the expanse of the valley and the span of the sky opened up as if it had all been hidden while we were driving, obscured by the close quarters of the interior. Nat handed one of the shovels to me without any words and he started off, crossing the road and up the grass hill. I followed him, glancing back to the truck as we hiked away. I saw the highway in the distance and a few lights from town, but the color was gone from the grass and the ground. It felt like I had been separated from the great open size of the land around us, that I had overlooked it somehow.

Nat propped his shovel up on his shoulder, blade back, and climbed quickly, reaching the top first. He stopped and looked out over the road and the truck below us to the valley as I caught up.

The ground was level on top and hard-packed by graders and machinery. Silhouettes of tractors, backhoe hookups, and front-loader buckets were clustered in dark shapes along the edge of the plateau, abandoned by their operators until morning.

"The house used to be up there," Nat said quietly, pointing beyond the equipment. He stabbed his shovel in the dirt and squatted down, leaning on the handle.

"They took out all the trees, the barns . . . I don't even recognize it."

He stared at the construction site, and I squatted next to him. I didn't know what we were waiting for. It was dark; we were alone. I wanted to say something. I felt I should comment on the view of the valley, but I knew he'd seen it. He'd seen it all his life.

I could see the outline of a portable rectangular office against the sky to our left, but there were no lights in it. I wondered if there were surveillance cameras or security dogs or maybe some other danger that he hadn't told me about. The uneasiness twisted in my stomach again, and my heart picked up. I wanted to go back. I thought of Julio shooting pool and the guys in town, my home and my parents – the whole life that was going on while I was out in the dark with Nat. I was stuck with him. There was no way to get around it.

He stood up and winced from being bent. Then without saying anything, he started walking across the flat toward the tractors. I followed him, focusing on the stripe pattern of his shirt as he picked up to a slight jog over the clay. The place

was foreign, and my perspective was lost in the dark seeing
the dim shapes of equipment and the faded skyline above
the hills. I started picturing what it might've been like, his
torn-down house, the barns, the life that grew up with it.
Images of his life jumped through me – horses and cattle,
births, death. The blood and bone that was in the ground,
muddy skulls and vertebrae, the mare buried in the earth.

He suddenly stopped, and my heart was strong. He stood
still, and I thought he had heard something. He looked left
and then right.

"I'm turned around . . ." he said in a whisper, moving
in circles, looking at the ground, then at the horizon, then
back at the ground.

"I can't . . . I think . . ." he mumbled, and then he
attacked the dirt with his shovel, wildly driving the blade
in. He stomped his boot down onto it and pried back on
the handle, scooping out a large chunk of earth, and heaved
it violently to the side. He dug in again and let out a grunt as
he heaved another lump of the clay, then drove the blade in
again, working at a pace that made him look like a younger
man in the dark. I fell in next to him and went to work.

We dug without speaking, matching each other in the
repetitive movement, feeling the weight of the caliche soil
in my back as we threw the shovelfuls. My forehead and
neck prickled and the sweat came, burning off the uneasiness
and allowing the work to take over. We struck hard at the
clay, digging in unison. He cursed at a scoop that came up

shallow, and he made up for it on the next strike, digging deeper and heaving the dirt randomly behind him. I looked at him, but I couldn't see his face in the dark, only his creased hat and his wild arms bending the stripes of his shirt. The smell of his cologne came in waves with his perspiration, and I kept my head down, watching my shovel sink into the black ground. Our tempo offset for a few rounds, and he threw dirt while I dug in – then we synchronized again, going back and forth like wiper blades. It felt urgent trying to keep up with his rhythm, sweat dripping off my eyebrows as I matched his rate. I was in a separate world with him that felt real in the smell of the earth and the weight of the shovel. I wanted to prove myself; I wanted to be there when he found her. It all seemed to come down to that, and the sweat and labor felt justified. My hands burned and my back hurt but I kept up with the old man, building a pile behind us.

We were knee-deep in a short time. The moisture grew in the deeper soil and the work became steadily harder, but we kept on, letting out groans that were soaked up by the pit.

Nat knocked against something. He scraped his shovel on it, then dropped down and pulled the heavy clay away with his hands.

"What is it?" I asked.

He threw a handful of rocks toward the portable office, and we went back to digging.

We worked for almost an hour, hitting rocks a few more

times. Nat threw them harder each time until he finally leaned back on the edge of the pit, and he took his hat off. He blew hard and wiped his pale forehead with his arm, looking down at our feet in the hole. He was worn out, and so was I.

"She shouldn't be this deep," he said.

He put his hat back on and climbed out.

Refilling the hole was easier. Shoveling the dirt back in took half the time, then we quit and walked back across the flat and down the hill.

Nat didn't say anything until we chunked the shovels back into the bed of his truck, and he handed me two tens from his pocket.

"I appreciate your help, Salvador . . . I wish I had a better idea of where she was up there. It's all so different now."

"It's no trouble," I said.

We made a three-point turn in the road, and he asked me if I would help him again some night. I knew he had been searching for a long time and would keep at it until he found her. I could see that.

The lights from town were far off as we headed back down the narrow road that edged the foothills. I looked at him across the seat, staring through the windshield wiping his mustache down over his mouth, and I told him I would. I knew it was the right thing to do, and I said I would.

A NOTE ON THE AUTHOR

Jesse Shepard lives in Northern California.

A NOTE ON THE TYPE

The text of this book is set in Bembo, the original types for which were cut by Francesco Griffo for the Venetian printer Aldus Manutius, and were first used in 1495 for Cardinal Bembo's *De Aetna*. Claude Garamond (1480–1561) used Bembo as a model, and so it became the front-runner of standard European type for the following two centuries. Its modern form was designed, following the original, for Monotype in 1929 and is widely in use today.

5   9/09/03